Presenting......

Corky's Five Minute Fairy Tales

A Collection of the 86 Most-Loved Fairy Tales

Written by: Patricia M. Fox/Shook

Assisted by: Emily Young and John Shook

Illustrated by: Corky Kennedy

https://fairytalemural.com

Corky's
Art°

To order a poster size print of the original mural, please visit

www.fairytalemural.com . A legend and game sheet accompanies

each print.

ACKNOWLEDGEMENTS

We wish to express our thanks and appreciation to all who previously told or wrote the now public domain fairy tales in order that we could write the stories depicted on The Fairy Tale Mural. We also wish to thank our grandmother, Eva Garrison Rockhill, for spending hours telling us stories and her mother, Corky Rockhill/Shook/Judson/Kennedy, for the eleven painstaking years it took her to draw and paint The Fairy Tale Mural.

Eva Rockhill 1897 - 1984

Cordelia Kennedy 1923 - 2014

Corky often appeared at grade schools. She would take the large mural, wear her Fairy Godmother dress and hat and point to the various pictures with her golden wand and tell fairy tales to the children. They loved it almost as much as she did!

TO THE READER

Some fairy tales are not for the faint of heart! They can be very graphic and scary for small children. However, in the time period when I grew up, most parents read fairy tales to their children, or told them the stories that had been passed down to them. Graphic, scary, or not, most of us seemed to thrive on them. However, parents may want to read through the stories before reading them to their children so they may have a say in what types of fairy tales they want their child to hear. A lot of how a child interprets a story, is in the way the parent reads it. The actions of the reader can make the story scary, silly, or outrageous! However you interpret or read these fairy tales, they are meant to be a fun way to interact with your child. These stories are condensed, as much as possible, so that most can be read in five minutes or less.

WHAT IS A FAIRY TALE, FOLK LORE OR A FABLE?

Although I didn't hear many fairy stories as a child, my husband's family grew up hearing and telling them on a daily basis. It was his mother and his grandmother's way of entertaining him because in those days, his father was away serving in World War II and there was no television, let alone computers. Entertainment for children was through stories, games, the radio and playing with friends, usually outdoors.

Fables are normally very short stories that have a moral to them, usually formed around animals rather than humans and usually teaches right from wrong. Many fables were made up by Aesop who was born about 620 BC.

A fairy tale can be very short or quite lengthy, but is meant to take your thoughts away from reality. The characters may be witches, fairies, elves, princes, princesses, queens and kings. They may be described by their profession, such as a shoe cobbler, the baker, the doctor, or just the old man or the pretty girl. In the past 200 years, many have been written down by such authors as The Brothers Grimm, Peter Ashbjornsen, Jorgen Moe, Charles Perrault and Hans Christian Andersen. It is hard to determine where some stories originated.

. Most fairy tales were handed down through the ages, perhaps starting with Adam and Eve telling Cain and Abel stories to keep them occupied. Many fables are attributed to Aesop. Charles Perrault, born 1628, is one of the first to get some stories written down. The Grimm Brothers were born in the 1780's. Rather than write stories, they collected them and put them into books. Since then, many others have written fairy tales. The stories in this book were put together to reflect the art work in The Fairy Tale Mural drawn by Corky Rockhill/Shook/Judson/Kennedy. Corky's mother, Eva Rockhill, a small southern lady, was a story teller extraordinaire, and the inspiration for Corky to draw the stories. A couple of these stories were possibly made up by her mother, Eva Rockhill, and not found elsewhere in print.

Many fairy stories usually begin with "once upon a time" and usually take place "in a land far away" and they are wrapped around imagination, magic and sorcery. Fairy stories can take a child to another plateau of "what can happen" when given a choice for good or evil acts. Fairy stories of long ago, were made to entertain bored children, or possibly put them to sleep, and today have been modernized into plays, movies, and even theme parks. Hopefully, it will take you or your child out of today's reality, possibly to a land far away for a short escape, even if only for a short time.

WHY WAS THIS FAIRY TALE BOOK WRITTEN?

Cordelia Jane Rockhill was always interested in drawing. As a child growing up in the twenties, and later as a mother in the sixties, Corky drew pictures for her own enjoyment. About 1965 one of her sons asked her to draw a picture of a giant so he could hang it on the wall of his bedroom. Then her daughter requested she draw a picture of a princess for her to hang on her wall, and so began The Fairy Tale Mural. It took her eleven years to draw the many pieces and eventually put them together into one 7-1/2' x 11-1/2' mural.

This work of art, which her family named "The Fairy Tale Mural", was duplicated in the 1970's as lithograph prints and sold to doctors' offices, hospitals and libraries in a 4' x 6' format. Eventually it was made into a 17-1/2" x 28" format so it could be made accessible to more children and later into 24" x 36" prints. More sizes are possible at some time. Coloring books may be the next item to come! Please check www.fairytalemural.com for our products.

This book has all the fairy tales depicted on the Fairy Tale Mural. There is a Legend in the book so if you have a print, you can find the pictures which go with the various stories. The stories are in alphabetical order, but to match the story to the picture, you can use the number in parenthesis to help you find it on the Legend, so you can find it on the mural.

Corky drew 86 fairy tales, but one of them, Pinocchio, got left off the Legend. If you have a print, it may be easy, or very hard, but if you search, you can find Pinocchio. I have listed Pinocchio as number 86 in the stories.

Corky was born in 1923 and died in 2014. She married three times. You may find her name many ways, i.e., Cordelia Jane Rockhill, Corky Shook, Corky Judson and Corky Kennedy.

The original Fairy Tale Mural consisted of 21 separate pieces drawn over a period of 11 years. Here all 21 pieces are shown together on a display board.

Emily Young with brother, John Shook, holding a copy of a 17-1/2" x 28" print. Various sizes of the print are available at https://fairytalemural.com. The Legend and Game Sheets will accompany each poster.

TABLE OF CONTENTS

STORY	LEGEND NO.	PAGE NO.

Corky, the artist, with the original Fairy Tale Mural. Her grandson, Scott Shook, is standing beside her. Directly across is grandson, John F. Shook and one of their good friends, Connie Davison Nusbaum. This was taken about 1972 while the 4' x 6' prints were being printed and sold.

Corky Rockhill Judson with her mother, Eva Rockhill, about 1972. Both were fantastic storytellers!

Use this Legend to find where the fairy tales are located on The Fairy Tale Mural

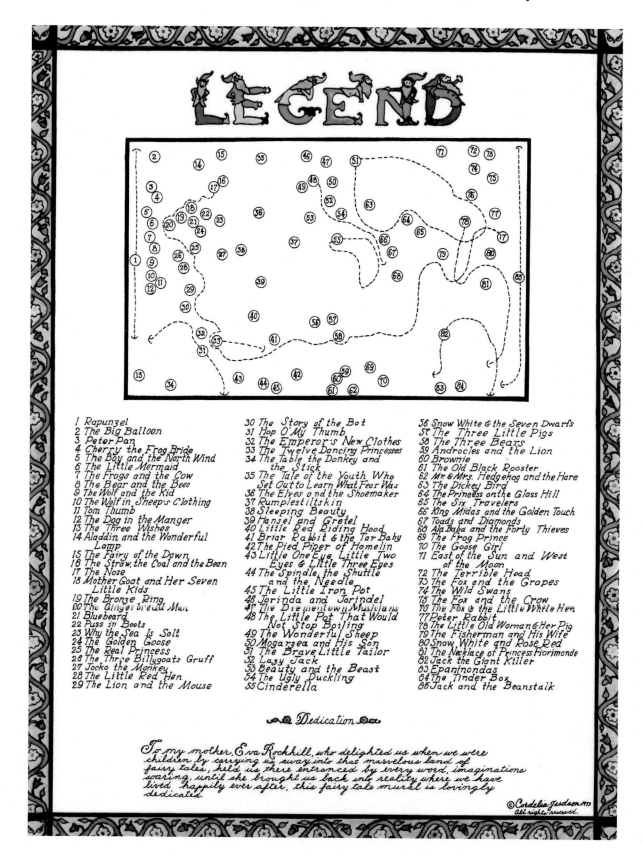

1 Rapunzel
2 The Big Balloon
3 Peter Pan
4 Cherry the Frog Bride
5 The Boy and the North Wind
6 The Little Mermaid
7 The Frogs and the Cow
8 The Bear and the Bees
9 The Wolf and the Kid
10 The Wolf in Sheep's Clothing
11 Tom Thumb
12 The Dog in the Manger
13 The Three Wishes
14 Aladdin and the Wonderful Lamp
15 The Fairy of the Dawn
16 The Straw, the Coal and the Bean
17 The Nose
18 Mother Goat and Her Seven Little Kids
19 The Bronze Ring
20 The Gingerbread Man
21 Bluebeard
22 Puss in Boots
23 Why the Sea Is Salt
24 The Golden Goose
25 The Real Princess
26 The Three Billygoats Gruff
27 Jocko the Monkey
28 The Little Red Hen
29 The Lion and the Mouse

30 The Story of the Bat
31 Hop O'My Thumb
32 The Emperor's New Clothes
33 The Twelve Dancing Princesses
34 The Table the Donkey and the Stick
35 The Tale of the Youth Who Set Out to Learn What Fear Was
36 The Elves and the Shoemaker
37 Rumplestiltskin
38 Sleeping Beauty
39 Hansel and Gretel
40 Little Red Riding Hood
41 Briar Rabbit & the Tar Baby
42 The Pied Piper of Hamelin
43 Little One Eye, Little Two Eyes & Little Three Eyes
44 The Spindle, the Shuttle and the Needle
45 The Little Iron Pot
46 Jorinda and Jorindel
47 The Brementown Musicians
48 The Little Pot That Would Not Stop Boiling
49 The Wonderful Sheep
50 Mogazea and His Son
51 The Brave Little Tailor
52 Lazy Jack
53 Beauty and the Beast
54 The Ugly Duckling
55 Cinderella

56 Snow White & the Seven Dwarfs
57 The Three Little Pigs
58 The Three Bears
59 Androcles and the Lion
60 Brownie
61 The Old Black Rooster
62 Mr & Mrs. Hedgehog and the Hare
63 The Dickey Bird
64 The Princess on the Glass Hill
65 The Six Travelers
66 King Midas and the Golden Touch
67 Toads and Diamonds
68 Ala Baba and the Forty Thieves
69 The Frog Prince
70 The Goose Girl
71 East of the Sun and West of the Moon
72 The Terrible Head
73 The Fox and the Grapes
74 The Wild Swans
75 The Fox and the Crow
76 The Fox & the Little White Hen
77 Peter Rabbit
78 The Little Old Woman & Her Pig
79 The Fisherman and His Wife
80 Snow White and Rose Red
81 The Necklace of Princess Fiorimonde
82 Jack the Giant Killer
83 Epaninondas
84 The Tinder Box
85 Jack and the Beanstalk

Dedication

To my mother, Eva Rockhill, who delighted us when we were children by carrying us away into that marvelous land of fairy tales, held us there entranced by every word, imaginations soaring, until she brought us back into reality where we have lived happily ever after, this fairy tale mural is lovingly dedicated.

ALA BABA AND THE FORTY THIEVES (68)

Ala Baba was a poor man. He made his living by cutting wood in the forest each day. One day while he was cutting wood he heard horses coming! Since robbers often roamed the woods, Ala Baba did not want to be seen so he climbed high up into a tree and hid.

The men got off their horses right under the tree where he was hiding. Oh my, there were 40 of them! They parted the bushes near the tree, revealing a hidden cave with a door that had no handle. Their leader faced the door and yelled "Open Sesame" and a door opened! All 40 noisy men went through the door and it closed behind them. In a little while the men came back out and the leader shouted "Close Sesame!" and the door closed.

After they rode off Ala Baba climbed down, stood before the cave and said, "Open Sesame!" and the door opened! He walked into a very large room and gasped in surprise. There were large jars of gold, big baskets of jewels and treasure chests stuffed with more jewels and gold! He stuffed what he could into the bags that fit over his donkey's back, stuck a few sticks of wood on top of each bag so no one would suspect he had such a treasure in them! He cried out "Close Sesame," and after the door closed, he hurried home.

Arriving at home he showed his wife his treasures. "Let's count it!" she cried. Ala Baba assured her she could not count that high. He said they needed to weigh it, but they had no scales. "Your rich brother, Cassim, has scales," said his wife. "I'll run and borrow his scales, but I won't let him know what I need to weigh. He is so rich and mean that he might try to cheat us out of the gold," she whimpered. When she arrived at Cassim's house and asked for the scales, her sister-in-law immediately suspected something. What would they have enough of that they would need to weigh it? So she rubbed some fat on the bottom of the scales, hoping that whatever they measured might stick to the bottom of the scales. Just as she suspected, when Ala Baba returned the scales a piece of gold was stuck to the bottom! She ran with the gold piece to her husband.

Cassim was soon knocking at Ala Baba's door. He showed Ala Baba the piece of gold and demanded to know where it came from and why they had so much that they needed to weigh it. Ala Baba could not really hide this secret from his brother so told him all about the gold.

The next morning Cassim went to the cave alone and said, "Open Sesame." He hurried into the room and filled his baskets with gold. But as he went to leave, he could not remember the words to make the door open! He cried out all kinds of words like "Open Up!" and "Open Now!" and "Sesame Door!" but he just could not think of the right words. Suddenly, the door did open and in came the robbers! They killed Cassim and left his body there as a warning to any others who might try to steal their gold and treasures from them.

That night when Cassim did not return, Ala Baba's sister-in-law ran to him. Could he go and find Cassim? Ala Baba at once set off for the cave. He found his brother hanging from the ceiling, dead. He took the body home to his sister-in-law. "You must tell your trusted servant, Morgiana what has happened. Have her spread the news that Cassim is sick and about to die. Then tomorrow we can tell everyone that Cassim died because he was sick."

Morgiana was not only a good and trusted servant, she was very smart. She went to the herbist and asked to buy some special herbs for her master who was very sick. She was back the next day asking for more herbs that are only given to one that is near death. So when Morgiana told the people of the town that Cassim had died, everyone had expected it since the herbist had spread the word of Morgiana's buying the special herbs.

When the robbers went back to the cave and found the body gone, they knew someone else knew of their cave and removed the body. Their leader went to town to find who had last died. They learned that Cassim was the only person who had died in the town that week.

With Cassim dead, Ala Baba and his wife moved into Cassim's big house with Cassim's wife, their son Gemini, and their servant, Morgiana. The robbers knew Ala Baba was the brother of the dead man and figured he was the only one who now knew the secret way into the cave. The leader disguised himself as an oil merchant. He bought twenty donkeys and put two huge baskets on each donkey. In the first basket he put a jar of oil. The robbers each climbed into the remaining baskets. The leader led the donkeys to Ala Baba's new house late in the evening. "There is no room at the inn and I need a place to spend the night. May I stay here?" he asked. Ala Baba, being a friendly and courteous man, and not recognizing him as one of the robbers, bid him to come in for the night.

Cassim's wife and Morgiana, hurried about fixing a meal for their guest. The kitchen was getting dark and they tried to light a lamp, but it was out of oil. Their guest had said he was an oil merchant so Cassim's wife sent Morgiana out to the donkeys to get a bit of oil for her lamp. When Morgiana came to a basket and started to lift the lid, a voice asked, "Is it time to kill him now?" Suspecting what must be planned, she answered very quietly, "No, not yet." She went quietly to each basket and told each it was not yet time. At last she found the oil she needed from the last basket and returned to light the lamp. Then she boiled water, took it outside and poured the boiling water into each basket, scalding and drowning every robber. Now she had to figure a way to kill their leader before he perhaps killed her or Ala Baba or Cassim.

After Morgiana served the meal, she asked if she could entertain Ala Baba and the guest with a dance. They were pleased with the idea so Morgiana changed into a dance costume, complete with a knife which she hid beneath her sash. She came dancing, leaping and twirling before them. Then suddenly, she plunged the knife into the man's heart. Ala Baba jumped up in surprise, but Morgiana explained about the guest and his robbers out in the baskets.

Ala Baba was so pleased with Morgiana that he promised her any request she desired. Her only request was to marry Cassim's son. Gemini was pleased with her request as he had long been in love with her.

Gemini and Ala Baba buried all the robbers deep in the cave. Ala Baba told Gemini the secret to getting in and out of the cave. Since they were the only people left alive who knew how to get in and out and since they neither one ever let the secret out except to their children, to this very day, only they and their children and their children's children on down the line have been in the secret hidden cave with all its treasures.

The End

ALADDIN AND THE WONDERFUL LAMP (14)

Young Aladdin lived with his widowed mother. They were very poor people and did not know any of Aladdin's father's relatives. A wicked magician decided this was just the boy that might be able to help him. He knew of a treasured magic lamp that would not be magic for the person who first found and touched it, but would be magic after another person had touched it. So, he went to Aladdin's mother and said he was a brother to her dead husband and had come to see about Aladdin's welfare.

The false uncle took Aladdin for a walk out into the country for many miles. He told Aladdin to gather wood and they built a fire. But instead of fixing food for their lunch, the magician threw some magic dust into the fire and mumbled some strange magic words. The earth trembled and shook and then a small door opened in the dirt.

"Aladdin, climb down through that door and drop down to a small room. You'll find an old tarnished lamp. Bring it to me and we will become very rich! Wear this ring on your finger and it will help you find it! Aladdin did as he was told and lowered himself into the little room. He found the lamp and started climbing back up. The man yelled for him to toss up the lamp to him, but Aladdin did not trust this new uncle. "Pull me up first," said Aladdin. The magician had planned on getting the lamp from Aladdin and then slamming the door shut to leave the boy in the hole, but now he could see that he was not going to have the lamp without the boy. Angrily he slammed the door shut and screamed, "Just stay in there you selfish boy!" and stormed off down the road.

Now Aladdin was scared. He put his hands together to pray and unknowingly rubbed the ring. A genie appeared! "I am the slave of whoever wears the ring. What do you want of me?" Aladdin whimpered, "I want to get out of this hole and be home again." And the next thing Aladdin knew, he was back in his home, holding the lamp.

Aladdin told his mother what happened. They thought the lamp must be worth something. His mother told Aladdin to get her a cloth so she could clean the lamp and maybe they could sell it. As she rubbed the lamp, a cloud of smoke rose and a huge genie appeared. "I am the genie of the lamp. What do you need?" After seeing one genie already that day, Aladdin was not nearly as scared as his mother. Aladdin said,

"We need some food." At once, before them was a table spread with fine silver bowls heaped with food.

Aladdin and his mother knew the genie could bring them riches, but they were simple people and only wanted to live as they had, with maybe a little more food sometimes. From then on, if they really needed something, they would ask the genie, but only if they really needed something badly.

Time went by and Aladdin grew to manhood. He had seen the king's daughter from a distance and was in love with her, but poor people could not marry into the king's royal family. So Aladdin's mother asked the genie for a basket full of jewels and took them to the king to ask for his daughter's hand in marriage to her son. "If you bring me 40 more baskets of jewels, I will grant your wish." The genie provided the 40 bushels of jewels without a moment's hesitation. "Now, have a castle built on my land for my daughter," said the king and that, too was done in only a moment. And so the king granted Aladdin's wish to marry his daughter, and the wedding was performed.

When the wicked magician discovered Aladdin was married to the princess and still had the magic lamp, he went to their city with some new lamps. He stood outside the castle yelling, "New lamps for old lamps!" It just so happened that Aladdin was away on a hunting trip, but his wife was watching out the window. She had never been told of the magic of the old lamp, so she thought she would surprise Aladdin by trading his lamp in for a new one and she sent a servant out to make the trade. When the wicked magician got the lamp, he rubbed it and the genie appeared. "What do you ask of me?" The magician demanded, "Take that castle, the princess in it, and me to a faraway place," he demanded. Immediately the genie whisked the castle, the princess and the magician to a faraway place, and where the castle had stood there was now only a hole in the ground.

That evening the king went to visit his daughter and found only a hole in the ground! He sent for Aladdin. When Aladdin appeared before the king, he could not understand how his castle and wife could possibly be gone, but they certainly were. "You have forty days to bring her back or I will throw you into the dungeon" roared the king. Aladdin knelt to pray and as he did, he rubbed the magic ring which was still on his hand. At once the genie of the ring appeared. "What do you ask of me?" inquired the genie. "Oh, if only you could take me to my wife and castle," moaned Aladdin. When he opened his eyes again he was in his wife's arms.

Aladdin's wife told him all that had happened. They made plans. That night when the magician came in to his supper, she put some powder in his drink to make him fall asleep. Meanwhile, Aladdin had been all through the castle and found the lamp. As soon as the magician was asleep, Aladdin rubbed the lamp and told the genie, "Take my castle, my wife, and me back to where we belong. Leave the magician sleeping here alone on the ground." The next thing they knew, their castle was back in its rightful place and the magician was nowhere to be found. Aladdin took his wife to see her father and explained all that had happened. Then Aladdin and his wife went back to their castle to live out their lives together happily ever after.

The End

ANDROCLES AND THE LION (59)

Androcles was a Roman slave and each day he did as his master bid. He worked very hard all day, but was often whipped in the evenings, for his master was cruel and did not think any slave worked hard enough.

Androcles was determined to escape, but knew if he was caught he would be put to death. One night he slipped quietly away. He walked for many miles and at last came to a cave where he lay down and fell fast asleep.

A noise woke him and he sat up. There stood a huge lion! Androcles shrunk back in terror and waited for the lion to kill him, but the lion only stood there and lifted one paw. The paw was swollen and bleeding and had a big thorn sticking in it. The lion was in pain and only wanted help. Androcles went to the lion and pulled the thorn from his paw. Then he wrapped the paw with his shirt to make it stop bleeding. The lion lay down next to Androcles and they both slept.

The next morning the lion limped out. He returned in a few minutes with a dead rabbit which he laid at Androcles' feet. The lion and Androcles became friends. They hunted and played together for three years. But Androcles grew lonesome for human companionship. He wanted to be with his own kind. He hugged the lion, said goodbye, and set off for the city.

It didn't take Androcles long to be caught. He was taken to the Emperor and sentenced to fight wild beasts in the arena before a crowd of spectators with only a spear. If he happened to live, he would be freed, but how would he stand a chance among wild beasts?

Androcles lived in a small room for two weeks, then one day he was given a spear and led into the arena. He stood there trembling. A gate opened and out ran a lion, roaring as loud as it could. The lion ran around the arena and straight at Androcles, then stopped. Suddenly the lion lunged at Androcles, but instead of attacking, he jumped on Androcles, wagged his tailed and licked Androcle's face! It was the same lion that Androcles had lived with for three years! The Emperor and the spectators clapped loudly. They released Androcles and the lion and from then on, the lion went everywhere with Androcles, wagging his tail and walking beside him like a faithful dog.

The End

BEAUTY AND THE BEAST (53)

A shipping merchant and his three daughters lived in a big mansion. They had plenty of money and wanted for nothing. The man loved all of his daughters, but his youngest, Beauty, he loved the most, for not only was she beautiful, but she was kind and never complained about anything, though her sisters did. Beauty loved life, no matter what it brought.

One day a courier came and told the merchant, "Sire, all your ships were lost at sea in a typhoon!" The merchant was shocked! He had spent all his money buying the cloth and spices that were on those ships. Now he was ruined.

They could no longer afford to stay in their mansion and have servants, so they moved into a small cottage in the country, not that Beauty minded. Though her sisters complained endlessly about not being able to live in a fine mansion and buy all the fine clothes they wanted, Beauty was just as happy as before. She planted flowers and a vegetable garden. She loved keeping the cottage tidy and clean and sang all day as she worked.

After many months of living in the cottage, another courier came one evening with word that one of the ships had been found washed ashore. It still had all the cloth and spices on it, so they were not completely ruined. Beauty's father would leave the next day and go to the city for his ship.

Before leaving he asked each of his daughters what he could bring back to them. The first daughter asked for five precious jewels so she could adorn her hair and fingers. The second daughter asked for seven new dresses, one for each day of the week. Beauty only asked for a rose.

The merchant went to the city and claimed his ship. It would provide enough money to get them going again. He bought his daughters the jewels and dresses they had asked for and headed for home. He knew he would find a rose somewhere along the way in the forest. He rode for many miles through the forest and when he was almost too tired to go any further, he came upon a castle. He could spend the night there.

He knocked at the door and it swung open on its own. He walked in and though no one seemed to be around, there on a table was spread a fine meal. He heard a voice say, "Be seated and eat what you like." He still saw no one around, but sat down and ate his fill. Upon finishing the meal a voice spoke again, "Rest yourself for the night, for you are welcome here."

The next morning the table was again spread with a fine meal, though he still saw no one. He ate his meal, retrieved his horse and made ready to leave. There by the gates he saw a beautiful rose bush. Whoever had fed him so well would surely not mind if he took one rose, so he picked just one. Thereupon a beast with the body of a man, but the head of a lion with horns, jumped upon the merchant. "How could you steal my roses when I have welcomed you into my home?" screamed the beast.

The frightened merchant tried to explain as best he could about what had happened to him and about how his daughter had only wanted a rose. The beast calmed down with the explanation, but then it demanded that rather than kill this man for stealing, the man should go home and send his daughter, Beauty, to live here with him. She would want for nothing.

The merchant went home sadly. How could he give Beauty to this beast? Yet the beast seemed like a kind enough animal. Upon arriving home he told Beauty the story and at once, she insisted she would go to the castle. She could not bear the thought of her father losing his life.

The next day Beauty went to the castle and received the same kind of treatment as her father. For the first two days she ate, rested, walked through the gardens, yet never saw anyone. On the third day the beast came to the evening meal. Beauty gasped and turned her head away when she first saw him, such an ugly thing he was! But the beast did not try to touch her. He only ate his meal and left, never saying a word. This went on for the next few weeks. The beast only came at the evening meal, ate, and left without speaking.

One night, Beauty could not bear the silence any longer and she said, "I wish you would talk to me for I am very lonely." And the beast answered, "Anything you wish is instantly granted." From that night on, they always talked, but Beauty could not get over the sight of his ugliness. He was very kind, but to see him always shocked her.

Still, seeing the beast only each evening, Beauty was lonely. One evening she said she wished she could go and visit her family. The beast replied, "I told you, all you have to do is wish, and it is granted at once. If you stay away more than two weeks, though, I shall die from loneliness for you. When the two weeks are up, just wish to be here and you shall be." And suddenly, she was in her own cottage again.

The two weeks went by so fast that Beauty could not believe it when the time was up. Surely he wouldn't mind if she stayed on another day. After two weeks and two days, she thought she should go back to the beast, for he had been good enough to let her go, and she found herself actually missing him. So at last she wished herself to be back with the beast and instantly she was back in the castle.

But at the evening meal, the beast did not appear. Beauty could not understand. She had missed the beast more than she imagined during the two weeks, but why was he not here now? Surely he could not really die of loneliness?

She went searching through the castle and finally out into the garden. She found him lying on the ground by the rose bush. He was dying! "I told you I would die of loneliness if you were gone for more than two weeks," he said sadly. "Oh, Beast, do not die! I have come to love you and could not bear life if you died!" she sobbed. At once, the beast changed into the most handsome man she had ever seen! The beast stood up and took Beauty in his arms and told her that he had been bewitched by a wicked witch many years ago. He had to stay in his beastly form until one day he would find a woman who could love him in spite of his ugliness. From that day on, the beast kept his handsome, human form, and he and Beauty were married and lived happily ever after.

The End

BLUEBEARD (21)

Bluebeard was a very rich man. He had many fine houses and lots of gold and silver. He had a blue bear though and the women ran away from him, thinking him strange and ugly.

Bluebeard desired to marry a neighboring lady. She, like the other women, thought him too ugly to ever marry. To gain her affection, he invited her and all her friends to a party. After much dancing, drinking and merriment, the woman decided that at least he was very rich! Even though she had heard stories that he had married several times and each wife had somehow disappeared, she decided to marry him.

After their marriage, the husband told her of his plans for a trip he must take. "While I am gone, you must make merry, for I would not have you lonely. Take these keys. This one opens my strong box. This one opens all my fine houses. This one gold key is to the closet at the end of the hall in the great house. I forbid you to enter this one closet, but all else is yours to play with and do as you please." After exacting her promise to stay away from the closet at the end of the hall, he left on his trip.

No sooner had he gone than the young wife decided she must look in the closet. She went down the hall and stood outside the door. She had promised not to enter that one little closet, but the temptation was too great. She opened the closet door and stood there in shock. All around the little room lay dead bodies. Blood was everywhere.

In her fright, she dropped the key. It was immediately soaked in blood. When she returned to her room she tried to wipe the blood from the key. But try as she would, the blood simply would not come off.

When Bluebeard returned he asked to have his keys back. "Why is there blood on this key?" he asked. "I don't know," said the trembling wife. "Of course you know! You went into the closet that I forbid, and for that I must kill you!" he shrieked. "Oh, please let me have a few moments to myself, so I may say my prayers," begged the young wife, hoping to stall him and possibly escape.

"Only a few moments, and then you must come down to me," he said. When she was alone, she cried out the window to her sister. "Sister Anne, go up to the tower and see

11

if my brothers are coming. They were to be here today. If you see them, make a sign for them to make haste!" Then she sat down and waited. From time to time she cried out to her sister to see if they were coming. "No, I don't see them yet!" was always the answer from her sister.

"It is time for you to come down now!" cried Bluebeard. "One more moment," begged the poor girl. "Anne, are they coming now?" she cried. "It looks like some men are on the road, but I cannot see who they may be," replied Anne.

"Are you coming down now, or do I have to come up and get you?" screamed Bluebeard. "One moment longer," she pleaded. As she knelt for a final prayer, Bluebeard broke through the door. As he grasped her by her hair she closed her eyes. "I must kill you for you have been into my secret closet!" he screamed. At that instant, when hope was nearly gone for the girl, her brothers ran in. They drew their swords and killed Bluebeard.

Bluebeard's death meant much money for his widow. After a time she married a poor kind man, making her rich, not only in wealth, but in happiness.

The End

BRIAR RABBIT AND THE TAR BABY (41)

Brer Fox and Brer Bear were always sitting around the woods and talking about how to get rid of Briar Rabbit. "That rabbit is a smart one, but he is just too bossy and pulls too many tricks on us." said Brer Bear. "I'm going to fix that Rabbit today," said Brer Fox. "What you going to do?" asked Brer Bear. "I'll show you," said Brer Fox and went to work. He made a shape out of some sticky black tar that looked sort of like a little boy. He even put a little hat on its head! "Now we just sit here and wait for that rabbit to come and touch it. Let's watch from the bushes. "

It wasn't long before Briar Rabbit came along. Briar Rabbit stopped and sang out "Howdy-do!" But the tar baby just sat there staring at that rabbit. "Hey, you going to say howdy-do to me?" asked Briar Rabbit. But the tar baby still just sat there. "Hey, be polite and talk to me or I'm going to smack you!" yelled Briar Rabbit. But the tar baby just kept sitting there, staring at that rabbit! Blam! Briar Rabbit hit that unpolite tar baby in the arm! "Hey, you better talk to me!" he yelled before he even realized he was stuck to the tar! "Let go of my fist!" he yelled at the tar baby. Then he tried to pull his hand out with the other hand and now he was stuck twice as bad. That rabbit got so stuck he couldn't hard move his eyeballs!

"Ha-ha!" Here came Brer Fox and Brer Bear jumping out of the bushes laughing like they were going to bust in half! "Ha-ha, we gotcha! Now we're going to roast you for our supper!" Well, now that rabbit was getting scared, but he was still awfully smart. Briar Rabbit, pretended to cry a little and said "Well, I guess I'm stuck and you got me where you want me, so you just go ahead and roast me, just please don't throw me in that briar patch!" say Briar Rabbit.

Brer Bear scratched his head, "Hold up, Brer Fox. It's going to be a lot of work to roast him. First we have to gather wood and build a fire and then we have to skin him to get that fuzzy hair off. It would be easier to just drown him!"

"Drown me, drown me dead, but please don't throw me in that briar patch," yelled Briar Rabbit.

"Hold up!" Brer Bear said. "To drown him we have to carry him down to the water and to hold him under we'll get our feet all wet. Let's skin him alive instead!"

"Skin me alive then! Chop off my head, peel my tail, but please don't throw me in that briar patch," begged Briar Rabbit.

"Oh, it's no fun to drown him or skin him if he's not scared," said Brer Fox. "He sure is scared of that briar patch though so let's throw him in there!" They yanked Briar Rabbit off the tar baby and flung him right in that briar patch!

Well, you should have heard all that noise coming from that briar patch. "Ooo! Oow! Ouch!" yelled Briar Rabbit. Pretty soon the noise died down and they thought he must be dead now. Then they heard a scrambling at the other end of the briar patch. Lo and behold Briar Rabbit came hopping out on the other side of the briar patch, way out of their reach, laughing at the top of his ears! "I told you don't throw me in that briar patch! You dummies, that's my favorite place! I was born in that briar patch. Look how it just combed that sticky black tar right off my pretty little fuzzy body!"

Brer Fox and Brer Bear just looked at each other and sighed as they heard Briar Rabbit go singing on down the hill!

The End

BROWNIE (60)

Some people do not believe in brownies, but let me tell you a story about a brownie that I believe in. This little brownie's name was Brownie! Isn't that a good name for a brownie?

Brownie lived in the coal cellar of a very big old house. He never came up in the house during the day for fear he would be stepped on, for he was only six inches tall. No

one in the house had ever seen Brownie, but the old cook and her kitchen helpers believed he lived in the cellar. Every night the old cook put a dish of mush behind the cellar door for Brownie to eat. The next morning the mush was always gone, so they had to believe in Brownie!

One day the old cook quit her job and the family hired a new young cook. She cooked almost as well as the old cook, but she was not a very neat person. She always left the supper dishes to be cleared away the next morning. The new cook did not believe in brownies and refused to put out the mush so the kitchen helpers had taken to putting out the mush, but one night, no one remembered.

That night when Brownie went to get his supper, nothing was there. "Where is my supper?" he asked out loud? Of course no one was there to answer for everyone was in bed. "Well, if no one is going to feed me, I shall go to the kitchen and find something myself," he said to himself, cause nobody else was listening! He slid under the door and into the kitchen. There he found the messy table that the cook had left full of dirty dishes. There were plenty of leftovers on the table, and Brownie just helped himself.

As Brownie hopped about on the table, he left little black footprints for his feet were not too clean because, now remember, he lived in the coal cellar. He noticed his footprints, but there was nothing he could do about them. He also saw a cat lying by the hearth watching him, but the cat did not seem to mind him being there and it just went to sleep.

When the cook came into the kitchen and found the black footprints the next morning, she did not know what to make of it. The footprints were too tiny to belong to a human but she certainly did not believe in brownies! Then she saw the cat lying on the hearth. She grabbed up a broom and chased the cat all around the kitchen yelling that it must never get up on her table again! That night she locked the cat in the coal cellar.

When Brownie woke that night and looked behind the door for his mush, again it was not there. He again crept under the door and into the kitchen and up on the table. Again there was a messy table; full of leftovers, for the cook knew that the cat was safely shut away in the coal cellar. Brownie had seen the cat, but he did not mind the cat sleeping in the cellar with him.

As Brownie hopped about eating this and that, again he made more little black footprints. He did not wish to be untidy, but this seemed to be the only way he could get anything to eat. The dog came into the kitchen for little while, but soon the dog lay down and went to sleep.

The next morning the cook found the tracks on the table again. She could not understand. She had shut the cat in the coal cellar. She opened the cellar door and the cat came purring out and rubbed her legs. Then who, she wondered? Certainly she did not believe in brownies. Then she saw the dog. She grabbed her broom and chased the dog about the kitchen. The dog went howling about trying to get away from her and her wicked broom. About then one of the kitchen helpers grabbed up the poor dog. "We have told you that the brownie that lives in the coal cellar must be fed mush each night. You would do better to put out the mush then to chase the poor cat and dog around!" she yelled at the cook.

Well that night, just to make sure, the new cook did put a dish of mush behind the cellar door. The next morning it was gone. The new cook never did quite believe in brownies, but she never did forget to put out the dish of mush each night after that. As she never saw any more footprints and the dish was always empty the next morning, who really knows for sure?

The End

CHERRY THE FROG BRIDE (4)

Cherry was a beautiful girl and was loved by everyone except an old woman that many people believed was a witch. The old woman hated Cherry because she was jealous of Cherry's beauty. One day three handsome brothers who were princes were passing through the town and saw Cherry drawing water from a well. "That girl shall marry me!" yelled all three princes at one time. As all three wanted to marry the same girl, each was jealous of the other and they began to fight among themselves.

The old woman (was she a witch?) saw the three brothers fighting over the beautiful girl and it made her angry. To have three men fighting over one pretty girl was too much for her and she cast a spell over the girl. "Cherry, vanish to the stream, for now you will be a frog, not a queen," chanted the old woman. At once Cherry vanished. Now we know the old woman was a witch! The three princes, no longer could see Cherry and they quit fighting and went their way.

When the three princes arrived home they were summoned by their father, the king. The king did not know which of his three sons to leave his throne to. He loved each of them equally and could not choose which son would make the best king. "I am going to give you three tests to prove which of you will make the best king," he said. "Each of you is to go your own way and bring back to me a piece of cloth five yards long that is fine enough to pass through the eye of a needle."

Where would they find such cloth? The two eldest sons took coaches and set about the land buying all the cloth. But the youngest walked drearily down the road. He came to a tiny bridge and sat down, moaning aloud about finding such a cloth. Just then a frog appeared with a very small piece of cloth in its hand and said, "I can help you." The young man just looked at the frog. No human, let alone a dumb frog, could possibly help him find such a cloth. "Trust me. Take this small piece of cloth to your father," pleaded the frog. The young man took the piece of cloth, for his older brothers had gone so swiftly in their coaches that they had probably bought up all the cloth in the land. This tiny, dirty piece of cloth would never do, but he could not go home empty handed.

The young man started home with the cloth in his pocket. Along the way the cloth grew heavier and heavier. When he reached home he found his brothers already there, having all their cloths tested, but none had been found yet that were able to pass through the eye of a needle. The young man pulled his cloth from his pocket. It was no longer a tiny, dirty, scrap of cloth. It was a beautiful white piece of cloth, as thin as a cobweb and exactly five yards long. It passed through the eye of the needle easily.

The king was delighted with his youngest son. But he had the next test ready now. "Go out and bring back to me a cat so small that it can sit in a thimble," said the king. "What? How could we find such a small cat" they all asked. But each of the sons started out as before, the two eldest in their coaches and the youngest on foot. The younger brother walked slowly back to the bridge. At least he could thank the frog for its help. Then he told the frog about his impossible task to find such a small cat.

"Oh, I can help you with that," said the frog. The frog fished its hand in the water and pulled out a worm and handed the worm to the prince. "Take this with you," said the frog. The young man looked at the frog as though it were crazy! "I said a cat, not a worm!" moaned the prince. But the frog simply said, "Do as I say and take the worm to your father." Well, the frog had helped him once, so the prince decided to trust it again.

When the prince arrived at the palace his brothers again had arrived, but none of their cats, not even the smallest kitten, could possibly sit in the thimble. The prince pulled the worm from his pocket and to his delight found that it was no longer a worm, but a very teeny tiny cat! The tiny cat easily sat in the thimble!

The king was delighted with his youngest son. But there was one more test, still. "Now go out and bring back the most beautiful girl in the land," said the king.

This time the brothers did not lose any time jumping into their coaches and racing off. But the younger brother took the same road as before. He raced back to the bridge and called out to the frog, "Can you tell me who is the most beautiful girl in the land? I must take her back to my father, the king!" The frog looked at the prince with sad eyes. Then it replied. "I cannot tell you, but I will show you. Go home and do not question what follows you," said the frog quietly.

The prince started down the road toward home. Once he looked around but all he saw were eight white mice dragging an apple and the frog hopping along behind. When the prince rounded the castle gates he could not see the procession behind him for a few moments. Suddenly around the gates came a beautiful coach drawn by eight white horses. Inside sat the lovely girl he recognized as Cherry, the girl he had fought over with his brothers. He climbed in beside her.

The king stood in awe when he saw Cherry. She surely was more beautiful than any of the girls that his other two sons had brought back with them. He at once announced to all who could hear that Cherry and his youngest son would now marry and they would now rule the land as the new king and queen.

The End

CINDERELLA (55)

Once upon a time a young girl lived with her stepmother and two ugly stepsisters. They were all very mean to her and nicknamed her Cinderella because she spent so much time working with the fireplace cinders. They made Cinderella do all the work around the house while they sat around eating candy and talking about how pretty they were. Actually Cinderella was the sweetest and prettiest girl in the whole land, but who would know that with all the cinders in her hair and the rags she had to wear. She had no pretty clothes like her stepsisters.

One day the king announced there would be a grand party at the palace so his son, the prince, could choose a wife. Every girl in the land was invited. When the two stepsisters heard this they laughed at the idea of Cinderella going. "After all," said one stepsister, "you have nothing to wear but rags!" "Of course she could go in her rags, but she could never wash all the cinders from her hair!" laughed the other ugly stepsister.

Cinderella helped them with their pretty clothes, put their hair up in curls and ran all over the house fetching fans and jewelry. She told her stepsisters they looked lovely, but there was no way to make such cruel, ugly girls look really pretty, no matter how hard she tried.

Her stepsisters left for the ball. Poor Cinderella sat by the fireplace and wept. She would have liked to go to the ball just to get out of the house and have some fun. Suddenly, a beautiful lady appeared in a pretty light blue dress. She carried a golden wand and she even had pretty wings! "Who are you?" asked Cinderella. The pretty lady answered, "I am your fairy godmother and I am going to see to it that you go to the ball. Run and fetch me six white mice, a large pumpkin and three lizards." Cinderella didn't know why the lady told her to do that, but she always did as she was told.

The fairy godmother touched her golden wand and whispered magic words and the white mice changed into horses, the pumpkin became a carriage and the lizards were now coachmen! She turned to Cinderella. "Now you must have a beautiful dress." She waved her wand over Cinderella's rags and they turned into the most beautiful pink dress that you have ever seen! She even had tiny glass slippers on her feet! As the coachmen helped her into the pumpkin carriage, the fairy godmother warned her, "You must be home by midnight or everything will turn back into the way it was. Remember, midnight."

When Cinderella entered the ballroom, everyone stopped and stared. No one knew who she was, but she was so beautiful! Her dress was beautiful, and her hair so perfect that even her stepsisters did not recognize her. The prince looked at her and immediately fell in love with her. He went to her side and asked her for the next dance.

They danced the rest of the evening together, and the prince never left her side. Cinderella did not tell him her name, for she knew that tomorrow she would be the same poor girl in rags, but, for tonight, she was so very happy.

The evening passed quickly and then Cinderella saw that it was five minutes before midnight. She ran from the room and down the stairs. In just five minutes her white horses would become white mice and her gown would become rags. In her haste, she lost one of her glass slippers on the steps of the palace. The prince ran after her, yelling for her to stop, but she kept running, jumped into the carriage and was off! All the prince had left of her was the tiny glass slipper.

The next day the prince took the glass slipper and went from house to house. As he entered each house he said, "Whoever can wear this slipper shall be my wife." Every girl in town tried to get her foot into the slipper, but no girl could get it on over her toes.

Finally he came to Cinderella's home. She watched from the kitchen as her stepsisters wriggled their toes and squirmed around, but they could not get the slipper on. Then Cinderella came from the kitchen and asked, "Please, may I try the slipper?" Her stepsisters laughed at her, but the prince took the slipper and slipped it onto Cinderella's foot. "Was it really you that I danced with at the ball?" he asked. "Yes and here is my other slipper to prove it," she answered. And suddenly her fairy godmother appeared and turned her rags into the same beautiful pink dress. "Cinderella, please come with me to the palace and become my bride," begged the prince.

Now that Cinderella was to marry the prince, the two stepsisters and their mother dropped to their knees before Cinderella. "Oh, please forgive us for treating you so badly," they begged. Cinderella was such a sweet and forgiving girl that she forgave them immediately. "Of course I will forgive you. You have taught me many things about working in this life. If my husband also wishes it, you can come to live at the palace with us. I will be better able to understand the people about me," said Cinderella. Then she left with the prince and they were soon married and they both lived happily ever after.

The End

EAST OF THE SUN AND WEST OF THE MOON (71)

There was once a poor man with many children. One night there came a tapping on the window. When the man went out to see who was tapping on this window, there stood a huge white bear. "If you will give me your youngest daughter, you shall never want for anything more in your life," said the bear. "Come back next week and I will give you an answer then," said the poor man.

The poor man told his youngest daughter what the bear said. They reasoned that as much as they would all miss each other, she should do this for her family. The bear also said the girl would never want for anything as long as she was true to him. The pretty girl decided she must do this for her family.

The next week the bear came to her. She climbed on his back and they were off. When they came to a mountain the bear knocked on the side of the mountain and a door opened upon the most beautiful castle. "I will not be around often, but if you need me, I will be nearby," said the bear and he left her. That night she went to her new bedroom. As she lay in the dark a man came to lie beside her. In the morning, he was gone. This happened each night. She would spend the day alone, and at night, after the light was out, a man would come and lie beside her. He was always gone when she woke, so she never saw what he looked like.

One day she called the bear to her. "I am so lonely. May I please go visit my family? Yes," said the bear. "But you must promise not to speak to your father alone. If you speak to him alone we shall both end up unlucky." She promised and they left at once. The bear left her with her family and called out that he would be back in two days, and to remember her promise.

Her family was so happy to see her. Their poor home was now a fine place. The furnishings were the finest and there was plenty of good food and clothing for all. Everything was just as the bear had promised. She spent the first day visiting and having fun with her family. The next day, her father came to her and wanted to speak alone with her. The girl put him off and her father was hurt. "Since you are gone you cannot now give your poor father just a few moments alone?" This made the girl feel badly and she decided she owed her father the truth. She told him all about her new home and about the man that came each night that she had never seen. She wanted so badly to see the man. "Take this candle and when he is sleeping, light it and you may see what he looks like," said her father.

That night when the girl had gone to bed, the man came and lay down beside her. When she was sure he was sleeping, she lit the candle and saw that he was the most handsome man she had ever seen. She could not resist bending over to kiss him. As she bent, three drops of wax dropped from the candle onto his shirt. He woke immediately. "You broke your promise and talked alone with your father. You have now made life unlucky for both of us. I had a curse put upon me that makes me a bear by day and a man by night. Had you held out for only a year, I would have been freed of the curse. Now I must leave you and go to the castle that is East of the Sun and West of the Moon, where the woman is that put this curse upon me. I will have to marry her daughter who is very mean and ugly. The girl wept. "Can't I come with you?" she cried. "No, you cannot come with me, but if you can find me after I am there, we may have a chance," he said.

She waited for two days and then set out to find him. She stopped when she saw an old lady. "Can you tell me how to get to the castle that is East of the Sun and West of the Moon?" she asked. "No, replied the lady, "but take this golden apple and go ask my neighbor. Perhaps she can help you." At the next house she asked the lady, "How can I find the castle that is East of the Sun and West of the Moon?" "I do not know, but take this gold comb and go ask the East Wind," replied the lady.

The East Wind was not much help either. He gave her a spinning wheel to take with her and told her to visit his cousin, the North Wind, who was very smart.

Upon reaching the North Wind she asked him, "Can you tell me how to get to the castle that is East of the Sun and West of the Moon?" "Well, it has been a very long time since I was there, but I think I can take you. Hop on my back and we'll go now," he replied. He sucked in all his air until he was very black and puffy and then blew it all out and they blew off. After several days of blowing around they finally came to the castle. He let her off and handed her the golden apple, the golden comb and the spinning wheel and left her there.

What should she do now? An ugly girl came up to her. "How much do you want for the golden apple?" "Oh, it is not for sale, but I'll give it to you if you will take me to the man who lives here tonight while he is in his room." The girl agreed.

That night the ugly girl took the pretty girl to the man's room and left. He was sleeping so soundly that she could not waken him even with all her poking and tickling. She begged and she wept, but he would not waken. In the morning the ugly girl told her it was time to leave, but she would let her come back again if the pretty girl would give her the golden comb. And it was agreed.

That night went the same. She could not waken him no matter how she tried. When the ugly girl came to tell her it was time to leave, she told her she could return that night again if she would give her the spinning wheel. It was agreed.

Meanwhile there were some people in the room next to the young man. They told him the ugly girl was putting sleeping juice in his supper drink, so much so that when for the last two nights a young girl had begged and pleaded with him to waken, he had not. So that night the man did not drink his drink at supper.

When the pretty girl came to him that night he was wide awake. He was so happy to see her! "I have a plan!" he cried. "I shall tell them that if the girl is worth marrying, that she must wash out the tallow that you spilt upon my shirt. I can fix it so that she cannot clean it."

So the man went to the ugly girl's father and mother and told them the girl must wash the tallow from his shirt to prove she was worth marrying. The girl tried and tried, but the harder she tried, the worse the tallow spread. The girl's father even tried, but when he touched the shirt, it turned black as night. "Why, I'll bet that poor girl sitting outside the window could do a better job!" said the man to his wife. "Oh, just let her try! No one can clean this filthy shirt!" said his wife and called the pretty girl in. She picked up the blackened shirt. She dipped it in the water and gave it a couple of rubs and it turned white as snow! The father, his wife and their daughter were so angry that they ran out the door and were never heard from again. The man and the pretty girl, knowing the curse was over, left as fast as they could from the castle that was East of the Sun and West of the Moon.

The End

EPANINONDAS (83)

Epaninondas was a very good boy. He always did exactly what he was told. One day his mother gave him a cake to take to his grandmother and said, "Epaninondas, you take this cake and hold on real tight so you don't drop it." So Epaninondas held real tight to the cake, all the way to his grandmother's house. When he held it out to his grandmother she asked, "What have you done to that cake, child?" "I held it real tight, just like Mother said," answered Epaninondas proudly. "Oh, Epaninondas, you've held it so tight it's not fit to eat now. Next time your mother gives you something to bring, you carry it on your head so you don't squeeze it to death!"

The next morning Epaninondas' mother said, "Epaninondas, take this butter to your grandmother." Epaninondas remembered what his grandmother had told him about putting it on his head, so he put the butter on his head. But as he walked the hot sun began to melt the butter. When he arrived at his grandmother's house the butter was running clear down his face! "Oh, Epaninondas, now look what's happened! Next time your mother gives you something to bring, you wet a leaf and wrap it around it and then bring it to me," she said.

On the next day his mother handed Epaninondas a kitten and told him to take it to his grandmother. "Now you be real careful with that kitten." Well, Epaninondas wanted to be real careful with the little kitten like his mother said and then he remembered what his grandmother had told him. He found a huge leaf and wet it and then wrapped it around the kitten. When he got to his grandmother's house the poor little kitten was shivering from being wrapped in that wet leaf.

"Oh, Epaninondas, what will we ever do with you?" cried his grandmother. "By the way," she warned, "I just baked two nice pies. While you are here, you just be careful how you step in them." So while his grandmother was drying the kitten, Epaninondas, wanted to be sure to mind his grandmother. He walked over and looked at the pies and he very carefully put one foot exactly in the center of one pie, and the other foot exactly in the center of the other pie!

The End

HANSEL AND GRETEL (39)

Hansel and Gretel lived with their father and stepmother. Their father and mother loved them very much, but they were very poor and could not afford to feed them. The stepmother nagged at the father. "They would be much better off to die suddenly from the beasts of the forest than to stay here and starve to death slowly," she said to their father. He finally agreed that maybe it was best. "We'll take them into the forest tomorrow," he finally said. The children heard them talking. Gretel began to cry. "Oh, Hansel, what shall we do?" she cried. "Do not fear, Gretel, I will take care of you," said Hansel.

The next morning their stepmother gave them each a piece of bread and they all four set out into the forest. When they were very deep into the forest their father stopped. He built up a big fire and said to the children, "You two sit here and eat your bread then take a nap. We are going further into the forest to cut wood." Then he hugged and kissed both of them tenderly and left.

Hansel was not worried. He had crumbled his bread and dropped pieces of it along the way from their house. He thought they would be able to follow it home. When their father did not return, they decided to follow the bread bits home. They started off, but could not find any bread bits. "Hansel, the birds have eaten it all up!" cried Gretel.

"Don't worry, Gretel, we'll walk around until we find our way back home."

They walked through the forest, but only got more and more lost. They came upon a clearing and saw a house. It was made of gingerbread and candy! They ran up to the house and while Hansel broke off a piece of the gingerbread roof, Gretel nibbled on a piece of the candy door. Oh, it was delicious! They were so hungry!

Suddenly the candy door opened and an old lady walked out. "Why, you precious little children, how did you ever find me way out here in the forest?" she asked. "We're lost from our parents," answered Hansel. "Well, you just come in and spend the night with me," said the old woman. She brought the children in and gave them each a room to sleep in. In the morning when they woke, the old lady said to Gretel, "Get busy and fix your brother some breakfast for I aim to make him fat and eat him!" cried the old lady. She wasn't really a sweet old lady, she was a witch who had built her candy house to attract little children to it so she could eat them!

Each day the old witch went to Hansel's room which was more like a cage than a room. "Stick your finger through the door, Hansel, so I can see how fat you are today!" she always yelled. But Hansel was very smart. The old lady could not see very well, and each day Hansel stuck a bone through the cage instead of his finger. After a month of this the old witch decided she could not wait forever to fatten him up and yelled to Gretel, "Light the oven. I'll eat him today anyway." Gretel lit the oven. "Now, hop into the oven, Gretel, and see if it is hot enough so that Hansel will die quickly," said the witch. Gretel was smart, too, though. "I don't think I can fit into that small oven." "Of course you can, you stupid child, even I can fit into it, see?" and she bent over and stuck her head up close to the oven. Gretel pushed the witch into the oven and slammed the door shut. Then she ran and freed Hansel. They each stuffed their pockets with coins and jewels that the old witch had stolen from other people and set off for home.

When they finally found their way home, their stepmother had died and their father was so glad to see them. He had hunted and hunted for them. With their coins and jewels they had now, they would never be hungry again.

The End

HOP O' MY THUMB (31)

A long time ago there lived a man and a woman who had eight little boys. The youngest was not just little, but tiny. When he was born he was not any bigger than his father's thumb, so they named him Hop O' My Thumb. He never did grow much bigger, so the name suited him.

The man and woman loved their children dearly, but they had no food and no money and they could not bear to watch them starve to death one by one. After much discussion, they decided to take the boys into the forest and leave them. Much better for them to die instantly from an animal than to slowly starve to death.

The next morning the man and woman took their eight boys into the forest. When the boys were busy playing, the man and woman tearfully slipped away with a last look at their boys. When the children noticed their parents were gone, they all began to cry. All but Hop O' My Thumb. He had heard his parents talking the night before and had slipped away and put white pebbles in his pocket. He had dropped them all along the way that morning so all they had to do was follow the pebbles back home.

When they got home they sat outside the window and listened to their parents. Inside the parents were moaning. When they had arrived home that day a man who had owed them money for a long time had come by and paid them. They had rushed out and tried to find the boys, but hadn't been able to find them. They went home and bought food and now had finished their supper. "We have food now. Why, oh why did we leave the children in the forest today? Tonight they could have eaten. I would give my life to have my children back," wept the woman. The boys could not keep still any longer and yelled with happiness as they ran inside to their parents.

The money and food held out for a time, but then came the day the money and food were gone again. Again the parents thought it best to take the children in the forest. So the next day they took the boys to the forest again and sadly left. Hop O' My Thumb again overhead his parents and this time had dropped crumbs of bread along the way. But when he and his brothers tried to find the trail of breadcrumbs, they found birds eating the last of them.

The boys wandered through the forest all day not knowing which way to go. They were scared of the noises they heard and it grew dark. They came upon a house and knocked at the door. A woman opened the door. "Why are you here? Don't you know that a mean giant lives here who eats little children?" The boys were scared and started to run away when the woman said she could surely hide the boys for one night. The giant was gone for a little while, so the boys talked it over and decided to trust the lady.

Soon the boys had eaten a fine meal. When they heard the giant coming, the lady put all the brothers under a bed. The giant came in. "I smell children!" he said excitedly. But the woman said he only smelled the meat she had fixed for his supper. The giant searched through the house, sure he could smell children and it didn't take him long to find the boys and pull them out from under the bed. He pulled out his knife but the woman said he should not waste the meat she had cooked for his supper. "Leave the children for tomorrow," she said. The giant agreed to wait and told her to put the boys to bed.

In the same room there were eight little girls sleeping in another bed. They were the giant's daughters. Each girl had a sleeping bonnet and a gold coin on her head. They looked much like any other little girls, but the woman had told the boys that these little girl giants would grow up to be just as mean as their father. They had not eaten any children yet, but they had bitten many. When the giant was fast asleep, Hop O' My Thumb climbed out of bed and gently took the bonnets and coins from the girls' heads. Then he and each of his brothers put them on.

In the night the giant woke and went to check on his daughters. He could not see very well in the dark so he only felt for the bonnets and gold coins. Satisfied they were all there, he went to the other bed where he thought the boys were sleeping. "I could kill them easier in their sleep," he said to himself, and he pulled out his giant knife and slit their throats all at one time. In the morning when the giant went in to get the boys for his breakfast, he found them all gone and his daughters all dead. "They'll pay for this!" he screamed and ran out the door to find the boys.

The boys had nearly reached home when they saw the giant coming right behind them. "You guys run on home and I'll see what I can do to stop the giant!" yelled Hop O' My Thumb. The brothers gladly ran on. Hop O' My Thumb called out to the giant to make him follow him rather than his brothers. The giant ran straight for Hop O' My Thumb, but Hop O' My Thumb was so small that he easily hid from the giant. After a time the giant tired of the chase and laid down to rest. Soon he was fast asleep.

The woman had told the boys about the giant's magic boots, so Hop O' My Thumb gently slipped the boots off the giant and slipped them on his own feet. The magic boots immediately fit him. He ran as fast as the wind to the giant's house and told the woman that the giant had been captured by many mean giants and they were holding him for a ransom. Now the giant may have been mean to children, but he had been good to this woman. So the woman handed over all the giant's gold and silver to Hop O' My Thumb. He ran home with the gold and silver and the family never again had to worry about money to buy food with. They even used some of the money as a reward for anyone who could kill the giant. Many of the men in their little town teamed up and soon they had killed the giant and collected their rewards and no children ever had to be afraid of the giant again.

The End

JACK AND THE BEANSTALK (85)

Jack and his mother lived in a very small cottage. They were very poor and Jack's mother decided the only thing to do was sell their cow. "Jack take the cow to town and sell her for as much as you can," she said.

On the way to market, Jack met a man with three beans. "I'll trade these three magic beans to you for that cow," said the man. "Are they really magic?" asked Jack. "Indeed they are. Go and plant them and you will soon see their magic," answered the man. So the man took the cow and Jack took the beans home. Jack's mother was very angry. "How could you be so stupid as to trade our cow for three stupid beans?" and she threw the beans out the window.

The next morning, Jack was shocked when he looked out the window. Lo and behold! The three beans had planted themselves and had grown to a very great height! He woke his mother and they ran out to stare at the giant beanstalk. It was taller than the house and was stretching up as far as they could see! "Mother, please let me climb it to see how high it goes," begged Jack.

After much coaxing, his mother agreed and he started climbing. He climbed higher and higher until it last when he looked down all he could see were clouds beneath him. At last he reached the top and there stood a fairy by a castle. The fairy spoke to Jack and said, "Jack, a giant lives in this castle. Many years ago he stole from your ancestor a goose, a harp and lots of money. You should find them and take them home to your mother, for they are rightfully yours." And then the fairy disappeared.

Jack entered the castle doors and came into a kitchen. There was a huge giant sitting at the table with a goose. "Lay!" demanded the giant. The scared goose laid a golden egg! "Lay!" demanded the giant again and the goose laid another golden egg. Jack knew this was the goose the fairy had spoken of.

"Fe-Fi-Fo-Fum, I smell the blood of an Englishman!" roared the giant. Well that scared Jack! Jack ran very fast and hid in a pantry. He peeked through the keyhole and watched the giant. Finally the giant left the room and went searching all through the castle. He could not find any Englishman so he sat down, picked up a stack of money and began to count it.

Suddenly the giant roared out again, "Fe-Fi-Fo-Fum, I still smell the blood of an Englishman!" But he still could not find any Englishman, so the giant picked up a harp and took it to the table. "Play me a tune," demanded the giant. The magic harp began to play a merry tune. "No," he shouted. "Play me something soft and soothing!" The harp then played a soft lullaby, so soft and soothing that the giant went sound asleep.

Jack, seeing the giant sleeping, crept out of the pantry. He would get back what was rightfully his. He tiptoed over and picked up the goose, the money and the harp. The harp, not understanding why someone strange was carrying him, yelled out "Let me go!"

The giant awoke and started running after Jack but Jack was really fast! He reached the beanstalk and started climbing down, down, down. The giant was very big and slow and he could not keep up with Jack. As Jack got near the bottom he yelled out to his mother. "Mother, get the axe!" Jack's mother could see the giant and ran and got the axe and handed it to Jack as he jumped to the ground. Jack started chopping madly at the beanstalk. The giant was half way down when Jack cut through the stalk. "CRASH!!" The beanstalk fell to the ground. When the giant fell to the ground it made a great hole in the earth. The hole was so deep that the giant was never seen again.

Jack and his mother kept the goose and the harp but they used the money to help all the poor people in the land.

The End

JACK THE GIANT KILLER (82)

A long time ago, in the days of King Arthur, there lived a giant name Cormoran. He was about fifty feet tall and had a huge appetite. He went about the countryside killing the cattle and pigs to eat for his dinners. He had killed so many of the animals that the people knew they would soon not have enough for themselves to eat, yet no one was brave enough to try to stop or kill the giant.

One day Cormoran took the last of the cows from a farm where Jack lived. Jack was very angry and determined to kill the giant. He knew he was not strong enough to kill the giant in a fight, so he decided to outwit the giant, and kill him by trickery.

Jack went up the mountain where the giant lived and dug a huge hole in the ground. Then he covered it with sticks and grass. Then he blew his horn as loud as he could and the giant wakened. "Who dares to waken me so early in the morning? I will find and kill whoever is out there," roared the giant! The giant stomped out of his cave and ran right to the spot where Jack had built the hole and he fell into it and broke his neck.

The people of the land called Jack, "Jack the Giant Killer", after that. He was very proud of himself, and the people loved him for doing such a brave deed. They gave Jack a wonderful sword and a purple coat that made him invisible.

With a name like Jack the Giant Killer, another giant soon came to that part of the country in search of Jack. No one could kill him, thought this giant. When Jack heard the giant was hunting for him he knew he would have to kill this giant by trickery also. He didn't know what he would do, but he had to try something. Since the giant had never seen Jack, and would not know him by sight, Jack went to where the giant was staying. Jack knocked at the door and when the giant opened it, Jack pretended to be a beggar looking for a free place to spend the night. The giant was very cordial and asked Jack to come right in and eat supper with him. When Jack saw the pile of human bones over in a corner, he knew why the giant was so cordial. If he didn't do something soon, his bones would surely be there too.

The giant had a huge bowl of soup. He brought another, just as big, for Jack. Jack ate all the soup he could, but when the giant wasn't looking, he poured the rest of the soup into a leather pouch inside his shirt. Then he challenged the giant to a contest. "Go ahead, little one," laughed the giant. "Anything you can do, I can do better." So Jack slit

32

his shirt through with a knife and, of course, the hidden pouch that was full of soup. The soup poured out of the pouch! Well, the giant was not to be outdone. If this young man could do that, and live, so could he. The giant took a sharp knife and slit his own stomach, and then fell dead.

The people again rejoiced, until another giant came. This giant kidnapped the king's daughter, who was to have been married to a prince. Everyone called to Jack the Giant Killer. "Go to the giant's castle and kill the giant and bring back the king's daughter!" Jack didn't know how he would do it, but do it he must!

Jack put on the purple coat to make him invisible and slipped by all the monsters that were guarding the castle. When he got inside he took off the cloak. A bunch of animals, large and small, crowded around Jack. A small deer looked at Jack, and walked off. Jack followed the deer and it led him to the giant's bedroom where he lay sleeping. Jack drew his sword and in one swift blow, he killed the giant! As the giant died, the deer turned into the kidnapped princess. The rest of the animals turned into the people they had been before the giant kidnapped and bewitched them.

Jack took the princess back to the king and she and the prince were married. Jack fell in love with her sister and soon they were also married and were happy together for the rest of their lives. And no more giants ever came after Jack or the people in their country again.

The End

JOCKO THE MONKEY (27)

Once upon a time there was a monkey named Jocko that lived on a farm with his human family. Jocko was smart for a monkey, always doing or trying to do everything like the rest of the family. One day the mother gave the baby a bottle and put it to bed for an afternoon nap. Jocko wondered what was in the bottle. When the mother left the room Jocko reached into the baby bed and took the bottle and ran out of the house, away across the big farmyard into the woods. There he climbed a very tall tree and sat among the leaves so that no one could see him. He drank all the milk, ate the nipple off the bottle and then he threw bottle away, down to the ground below, where the bottle broke into many pieces.

Meanwhile back at the house, the mother kept hearing the baby cry and fuss, so she went in to see what was wrong. She saw the bottle was not there, so she looked under the covers, under the baby and under the bed. Then she knew. "Jocko!" she called. When he didn't come, she went out through the barnyard calling his name. She finally went into the woods and saw him hiding way up in the tall tree and saw the broken bottle at her feet? With her hands on her hips, she yelled, "Jocko, you get down here this minute! Right now!" When he came down she bawled him out and he behaved himself for some time after that.

One day the mother got out butter, flour, sugar, eggs, and all the ingredients needed to make a cake. She stirred the batter, poured it in the cake pans, put it in the oven and baked the cake. When it was done, she put icing on the cake.

That afternoon when the mother left the house, Jocko decided he would bake a cake. He got down a big pan, a dozen eggs, the big bag of flour, the butter, baking powder and everything he had seen her put into the batter. Then he dumped in the dozen eggs, shells and all, the bag of flour, baking powder, salt and sugar into the big pan. He made an attempt to stir it together, then shoved the big pan into the cold oven. When the mother came home she found a really big mess in her kitchen. Flour and eggshells were everywhere! Milk was spilled on the table and the floor. "Jocko! What have you done?" Jocko went to the oven and opened the door. There sat all the things in a big mess in the pan. Then she really scolded Jocko and made him stand in the corner to punish him.

Another day the mother had to leave the house again. Jocko was left alone, sitting in the kitchen. Things were very quiet and Jocko could hear the ticking of the kitchen clock. He wondered what was in the clock that was making the tick-tock. He climbed up on a chair, took the clock down and got a hammer to open the clock to find the tick-tock. He took the clock out on the porch and proceeded to bang on the clock until it was broken in all kinds of little pieces. He could no longer hear the tick-tock and figured he had fixed the problem. When the mother came home she looked up to see what time it was. Where was the clock? "Jocko! What have you done to my clock?" This time she put Jocko in a playpen for two hours, which he didn't like at all.

One morning Jocko went to the hen house with the mother in order to gather the eggs. When her basket was full she returned to the house and placed the basket full of eggs on the counter in the kitchen. Jocko had seen her disturb the hens from their nests to reach in and get the eggs. Jocko knew the hens sat on the nests to hatch out baby chicks. Later that morning, when no one was home, Jocko took the basket of eggs to the bedroom, placed all the eggs in a pile in the middle of the bed, and climbed up on them to hatch them into baby chicks. Of course he was too heavy and they all broke. When the mother returned home, she discovered the eggs were no longer sitting on the counter. "Jocko! Come here!" So Jocko came. "Where are the eggs I left on this counter this morning?" He took her hand and led her to the bedroom, and she saw the mess in the bed. Now Jocko was really in trouble! She chased him around and around the house until he fled to the hen house to hide, but the mother found him, took him to town and sold him. Now there would be no more monkey business ever again around that house!

The End

JORINDA AND JORINDEL (46)

Jorinda was a beautiful young woman who was soon to be married to a young man named Jorindel. They were very much in love and often went for walks in the woods. One day when they were walking in the woods and talking about plans for their wedding Jorinda stopped. "Jorindel, we must turn back soon for we cannot get too close to the witch's castle here in the woods. It is said that she turns men into statues and women into birds. Then she puts the birds into cages and keeps them." But Jorindel was not worried. He never worried about anything as long as he had Jorinda with him, and they continued walking.

Suddenly the witch was before them. "Ha-ha, you sillies. Now you are in my power and there is nothing you can do," she cackled. Jorindel wanted to grab Jorinda and run, but found he could not move. He could see and hear everything, but he could not so much as move his little finger. The witch turned to Jorinda and mumbled a few words. At once, Jorinda turned into a lovely bird. The witch grabbed the bird and put her in a cage she was carrying. Then she ran off into the woods. Jorindel still stood there like a statue. He wanted to run after them, but could not. He wanted to weep, but could not. He stood there all the rest of the day. Finally the moon shone upon him and he was freed. He could move again. He knew it would do no good to go after them now, for now he believed the story Jorinda had told him earlier in the day.

Jorindel spent many lonely weeks thinking about how to get back his lovely Jorinda. But, he could think of nothing that would work. At night he dreamed of the good times he and Jorinda had together. Then one night, he dreamed of a large pink flower. It was a magic flower that took him to the witch's castle safely and helped him to free Jorinda. The next morning Jorindel set out to find the magic flower he had dreamed of. He did not find the right flower that day, nor the next. In fact, he spent many days looking at every pink flower he could find. At last he found it! This was the magic flower in his dream! He plucked it and hurried off to the witch's castle.

As he neared the castle, he did not turn into a statue. He kept going until he was past the gates, and inside the doors of the castle. He heard the sweet sound of birds singing. He went through a door and there sat the witch with hundreds of birds in cages around her. The witch screamed, "Get out!" But Jorindel would not leave. The witch screamed all sorts of magic words trying to change him into a statue again, but she could not change him as long as he held the magic flower.

Jorindel went from cage to cage looking at the birds. Then he saw the witch running with one cage in her hand. Jorindel caught the witch and touched both the cage and the witch with the magic flower. The witch disappeared, the bird in the cage disappeared, and there stood his pretty Jorinda. Jorindel touched each cage with the magic flower and girls appeared where the birds had been.

Jorinda and Jorindel were married soon after that. They bought a bird cage and caught a lovely bird to put inside it to remind them of how they had nearly lost each other. They lived happily together for the rest of their lives.

The End

KING MIDAS AND THE GOLDEN TOUCH (66)

King Midas had a lovely daughter named Marigold. He loved Marigold more than life itself, and she loved her father just as much. Marigold often picked flowers and took them to her father. He would look at them and smile and tell her they were pretty, but worthless because the flowers would shrivel and die in a day's time but if they were gold they would last forever. Marigold always laughed at the little joke, not knowing her father really meant what he said.

King Midas collected gold and kept all his golden things piled in a secret room of the castle. One day he was in his secret room counting his golden pieces when a tiny, strange man appeared to him. How had the little man gotten into his secret room? "I am the Prince of Gold and have come to grant you one wish. Think carefully and tell me what it would be." King Midas did not know what to think of this stranger, but he did know what he wanted more than anything. "If you could really grant me one wish, it would be to have everything I touch turn into gold! Then I would be the richest man in the world!" The stranger warned, "King Midas, you will learn that gold is not the most precious possession, for after you waken in the morning, everything you touch will turn into gold."

The next morning when King Midas woke, he was so hot! His blanket felt like a heavy weight upon him. He was astonished to find his blanket was now gold! His bed and his pillow were also gold! How exciting! He grabbed his clothes and they instantly turned to gold! They were hot and heavy, but that was a small price to pay for such

lovely, golden garments. He started out his door and the doorknob turned to gold! He ran down the staircase and the staircase banister turned to gold as he touched it! Such a lovely thing! He ran straight out to the garden for he had always told Marigold that the flowers would be worth more if they were gold. Today he would prove it! He ran to each flower in the garden and turned each one to gold!

He went to breakfast and waited for Marigold. But as he touched his cup it, too, turned to gold! Then he picked up his water glass and it turned to gold! Now what? He was sitting there in his now golden chair thinking about what to do now.

Then Marigold came running in to him, weeping. "Father, the flowers are all ruined. They've turned to metal and they don't smell sweet!" King Midas didn't want to admit to anything since she was upset, so he told her to please quit crying and sit down and eat her breakfast. He would show her later that they were not really ruined, but better. Marigold, having all the faith in the world in her father, sat down to eat. Such a good father he was to her. She began to eat and noticed her father was not eating. "Please eat with me, Father," she said sweetly.

He tried again. He picked up his fork and it turned to gold! Then he stuck his fork into his eggs, and the eggs turned into gold. What was he to do? How was he going to eat? Granted, gold was the most precious thing, but how was he to eat it, and he was so hungry! Marigold had not noticed the golden cup, glass, fork and eggs. "Father, why do you not eat? Don't you feel well?" She ran to him and put her hand on his brow to feel if he was feverish. At once, she turned to gold!

"Marigold! What have I done to you?" he cried. Not for anything in the world would he have had this happen. His daughter was no longer a sweet little girl, she was now a golden statue! What could he do? He would trade all the gold in the world to have his little girl back again with her brown hair and rosy cheeks!

Then the stranger appeared again. "Have you found yet that simple things like a cup of water, a piece of bread, and especially a real child are more precious than gold?" The king wept and nodded his head. "If you are certain you want to give up this golden touch, take this pitcher, go to the river and fill it. Then sprinkle that water over anything you want to be changed back the way it was."

King Midas did not hesitate. He picked up the pitcher, which instantly turned to gold, and he ran to the river. He dipped the pitcher into the water and it turned back to its normal state, and he filled it with water! He ran back to Marigold and sprinkled her until she was soaking wet! Then he ran through the garden and sprinkled every flower. He continued running through the palace until he had turned everything back the way it was. Everything changed back like it was except for Marigold's hair. Where her hair had always been brown, it now kept its golden color! This must be meant as a reminder to him that gold is not the most precious thing in the world, and he gave away all his golden treasure to the poor people in this land.

The End

LAZY JACK (52)

Jack was a good boy, but very lazy. He spent all of his time sitting in the sun. One day his mother became very disgusted with him and said she would have to turn him out if he did not go to work and help to make them a living.

The next morning, Lazy Jack set out to find himself some work. He hired himself out to a farmer for a dollar, but on the way home he lost the dollar. "Jack," said his mother, "next time carry it in your pocket."

The next day Lazy Jack hired himself out again and was paid a jar of milk for his wages. Lazy Jack stuck the jar of milk in his pocket and set off for home. But by the time he reached home, all the milk had spilled out of the pocket. "Jack," said his mother, "next time carry it on your head."

The following day Lazy Jack worked for the cheesemaker for a piece of cheese as his day's wages. At the end of the day, the cheesemaker paid Jack with cheese and Jack put it on his head and started for home. When he reached home, the cheese had melted and was matted in his hair. "Oh, Jack," cried the mother, "what will you do wrong next? From now on, carry your payment in your hands."

The next day Jack went to work for another farmer. His payment that day was a kitten. Jack carried the kitten in his hands, like his mother said, but it got excited and scratched Jack and he dropped the kitten and it ran away. "Jack, Jack, Jack. You should have tied a string around it and dragged it home," said his mother.

He worked for a cattle keeper the day after and was paid with a piece of beef. Jack tied a string around the beef and dragged it, but when he reached home the beef was full of dirt and was ruined. "From now on, carry it on your shoulder," said his mother.

Again, Jack went back to the cattle keeper to work. That night the cattle keeper paid Jack with a donkey. "My goodness," thought Jack. "How do I carry this donkey on my shoulder?" Jack thought for a time and finally he stooped down under the donkey and lifted it up on his shoulders. He looked so funny carrying the donkey, just like when his father used to give him piggyback rides.

Jack trudged along toward home. On his way he passed the house of a very rich man who had a daughter who had been very sick. She had been so sick that she had been left unable to laugh. The doctor said that if anyone could make the girl laugh, she would be cured. And here came Jack carrying the donkey on his shoulders! The girl saw Jack and she burst out laughing! She laughed and laughed. Her father was overjoyed and ran out to Jack and invited him in. His daughter had been cured of her sickness because of Jack, so the rich man promised Jack he could marry his daughter and split his riches with him. Lazy Jack never again had to worry about money or payment or how to get it home.

The End

LITTLE ONE EYE, LITTLE TWO EYES, AND LITTLE THREE EYES (43)

There was once a woman with three daughters. The eldest was named Little One Eye because she had only one eye and it was right in the middle of her forehead. The second daughter was named Little Two Eyes because she had two eyes like other children. The youngest was named Little Three Eyes because she had three eyes. The mother and the other two sisters shunned Little Two Eyes because she was just like all the other children and she deserved nothing special. They made her do all the work around the house and take the goat to pasture every day. They gave her only scraps of food, so Little Two Eyes was always hungry.

One day Little Two Eyes was in the pasture watching the goat and crying. A fairy appeared and asked why she was crying. "I cry because I am hungry for I never have enough to eat," said Little Two Eyes. "Well, whenever you are hungry hereafter, just call your goat to you and say `Little goat, bleat, little table appear'," said the fairy. "When you are full, just say `Little goat bleat, little table away'."

Little Two Eyes was hungry so she tried it right away. "Little goat, bleat, little table appear," she said. Immediately before her appeared a table filled with a fine spread of food. She ate till she had her fill and then said, "Little goat bleat, little table away," and it went away. After that she was not hungry anymore.

Little Two Eyes started leaving the scraps of food that her sisters threw to her. Her mother decided she must be getting food elsewhere and told Little One Eye to go and watch her the next day. Little Two Eyes overheard them talking, so the next day when Little One Eye said she was going to go and make sure Little Two Eyes took the goat to the greenest pasture, Little Two Eyes knew why her sister was really going with her. Now Little One Eye was not used to walking all day and she grew tired and she lay down to take a nap. While she was sleeping, Little Two Eyes called out the magic words to the goat and ate her fill.

The next day Little Three Eyes announced she was going to make sure her sister took the goat to the greenest pasture, but Little Two Eyes knew the real reason she was going. When they got to the pasture, Little Three Eyes lay down and pretended to sleep,

42

but she kept watch with her third eye only half closed. When Little Two Eyes called the magic words to her goat, Little Three Eyes saw and ran home to tell her mother. The mother flew into a rage and killed the goat.

Little Two Eyes ran into the pasture to cry and the fairy appeared. "Go ask your mother if you can have the goat's heart for a souvenir and then bury it by the front door and you will have good luck," said the fairy. So Little Two Eyes went and begged to have the heart. When her mother and sisters were sleeping that night, Little Two Eyes buried the heart by the front door.

The next morning amazingly there was a huge apple tree right where she had buried the heart! Wow! "Climb it and get us some apples, Little One Eye," said the mother. Little One Eye climbed the tree, but every time she tried to pull an apple from the tree, it would not come off. "Little Three Eyes, you try," said the mother. Little Three Eyes tried, but had no better luck. Then the mother even tried, but also in vain. "Maybe Little Two Eyes can get them," laughed the sisters. As it turned out, Little Two Eyes was the only one who could pick apples from the tree.

One day a prince came riding by. "Oh, how I should love to have an apple. Whoever is the quickest about getting me an apple shall never want for anything," he said. Little One Eye and Little Three Eyes scrambled up the tree, but try as they might, they could not get one apple from the tree. "My gracious, cannot anyone get an apple from this tree?" he asked. "Our sister can at times, but she is so plain she rarely comes out of doors," said Little One Eye.

The prince called Little Two Eyes out and asked her if she could get him an apple. She climbed up and handed him down an apple. "What can I do for you?" he asked. "Please take me away from here for my mother and sisters do not feed me enough and I must do all the work," Little Two Eyes answered. The prince pulled her onto his horse and they rode off to his castle. They fell in love and soon they were married. Little Two Eyes' mother and sisters begged her forgiveness and she forgave them and let them live out their days with her in the castle.

The End

LITTLE RED RIDING HOOD (40)

There was once a sweet little girl who was loved by her mother and grandmother. The grandmother could sew very well and so she made her lovely little granddaughter a red cape with a red hood.   The granddaughter wore the red cape everywhere she went and people started calling the little girl Little Red Riding Hood.

One day the grandmother was not feeling well, so Little Red Riding Hood's mother gave her a basket of fruit and told her to take it to her grandmother in the woods. "Now

go with haste, but not so fast that you might trip and fall. Do not stop to pick flowers or talk with any strangers, but go straight to Grandma's house," said her mother as Little Red Riding Hood started down the path to the woods.

Little Red Riding Hood skipped along merrily on her way and soon met up with a wolf. "Good day little girl," he said cheerily.   "Where are you going?" Now she knew she was not supposed to talk to strangers, but he seemed so nice that she thought he could not hurt anyone. "I'm on my way to my grandma's house for she is sick and I'm taking her some fruit," she replied sweetly.

Now the wolf was really a mean one and thought the little girl would surely make a tasty meal. "Why don't you pick some flowers to take to your grandmother? That would surely please her," said the wolf. Little Red Riding Hood remembered that she was not to pick any flowers, but she thought that the pleasure they would bring her grandmother was surely worth the little time it would take to pick some. So she stayed and picked a few flowers and the wolf went off down the path, straight to Grandma's house. When he got there he tied up the poor sick lady and put a handkerchief in her mouth so she could not cry out. Then he put her in the closet.

A few minutes went by while the wolf changed into Grandma's nightclothes and put on her glasses and jumped into her bed. Just then Little Red Riding Hood knocked at the door. "Come in," squeaked the wolf in an imitation voice of Grandma. Little Red Riding Hood walked over to the bed. "Grandma, you must really be sick! You don't look yourself at all today! How big your eyes are!" "The better to see you with, my child," said snickered the wolf.

"But Grandma, what big ears you have," said the little girl. "The better to hear you with," whispered the wolf.

"But Grandma, what a big mouth you have!" "The better to eat you with!" screamed the mean wolf as he leaped from the bed and chased Little Red Riding Hood all around the room.

Now Little Red Riding Hood was not about to be eaten by any wolf and she ran and screamed at the top of her lungs! Surely somebody would hear her and come to help! And she was right. Not far away a man was chopping wood and heard her cries for help. He ran to the house and flung open the door. It only took a moment for him to fling his axe at the wolf and kill him! He wouldn't be trying to eat any little girls again!

Grandma had heard all that had gone on and was wriggling all around the closet making muffled noises. The woodsman opened the closet door and found her. They let the grandmother out of the closet and untied her.

When Little Red Riding Hood went home, she did just as her mother had told her. She went straight through the woods without stopping to pick flowers or talk to any strangers. She had learned her lesson and would pay more attention to what her mother told her from now on!

The End

MOGARZEA AND HIS SON (50)

There was once an orphan boy. His guardian was a mean man so the boy set off to find a place for himself. He walked over hills and swam streams till he found himself deep in the woods. All around was dark except for a tiny spot of light. He followed the light, which turned out to be a fire. A huge man, like a giant, was sleeping beside the fire. The boy lay down beside the big man.

In the morning the giant man was surprised to see the boy lying by him. "Where did you come from?" asked the man. "I came to you in the night and now I am your son," answered the boy. "Well, I am Mogarzea, and if you are my son, you must take the sheep to pasture," said the giant man. "Cannot you come with me, Father?" asked the boy. "No, and I will tell you why, " said the man.

Mogarzea told the boy that his father was an emperor. He had been on the way to the Sweet Milk Lake to marry one of the fairies who lived there when three wicked fairies fell upon him and robbed him of his land and his soul. He pointed out the land which had been his. He could not return to his land again and without his soul, he could not laugh.

The boy felt sorry for Mogarzea and swore to help him. Each day he took the sheep a little closer to the land of Mogarzea. One day the sheep began to wander onto the land. The boy followed them, playing his flute all the time. Three wicked fairies appeared and demanded he keep playing for them while they danced. They danced all day long. When it became late, the boy told them he must go. They made him promise to return the next day or they would put a curse on him.

That night the boy made a plan. When dawn came the boy left again for the land of Mogarzea. He played his flute all day for the fairies while they danced. When it was getting dusk he pretended to drop the flute, by accident, and walked on. In a few moments he ran back to the fairies and told them he had lost his flute and began to weep. He wept so hard that their hearts melted for him and they said they would help him make another. They had a tree that would serve well from which to make a flute. So they all went to the tree. The boy struck the tree with an axe and made a long crevice. "Put your fingers in the crevice and I will pull out enough wood for my flute," begged the boy.

When the fairies put their fingers in the crevice, the boy pulled the axe out and their fingers were stuck in the tree! They screamed and cried, but the boy would not let them go. "You must give Mogarzea his soul back," he yelled, "or I will not let you go!" And they agreed.

The boy ran back to Mogarzea and told him what had happened. Mogarzea ran back with him to the trapped fairies. The fairies told him to get the bottle where they had his soul trapped. Morgarzea ran to get the bottle and yelled so loud for joy that his soul jumped right back into him. Mogarzea then released the fairies and he and the boy left for the emperor's palace.

Mogarzea was so happy that he told the boy to name his price. The boy said, "Just show me how to get to the Sweet Milk Lake and I will go and take one of the fairies for a wife." Mogarzea explained the way.

The boy went to the Sweet Milk Lake and played his flute so sweetly that he soon had a beautiful kind fairy come to him. He took her back to the palace and they were married and lived out their lives with Mogarzea.

The End

MOTHER GOAT AND HER SEVEN LITTLE KIDS (18)

In a mountain region that was covered with woods lived seven little goat kids with their mother. The mother goat loved all her kids just as much as your mother loves you. One day she had to go into the woods to find something to eat for her kids. "Now, kids, you stay here in the house and do not open the door to anyone. You know that if the old wolf sees me leave, he may try to get to you. You will know him by his deep voice and his black feet. Do not let him in. I'll be back soon," she said tenderly and was on her way.

The kids played for a while and then someone knocked at the door. "Let me in kids, for I am home with good things to eat," said the deep voice. But the kids knew that deep voice must belong to the wolf. They shouted for him to go away. "We know you are not our mother for she has a sweet voice'" one of them shouted.

The wolf left, but he only went to his home and ate some sugar. Then he came back and said very sweetly, "Kids, I am home now. Open the door." One of the kids thought the voice was his mother's and went to open the door, but just at that time the wolf placed one of his feet on the windowsill. It was black! "No, no. Go away! Our mother does not have black feet and you must be the wolf again!"

The wolf stomped off very angry. He went back home and poured some flour over his feet and back he went to the kids' house. "Let me in kids. I am home now with your supper," said the wolf sweetly. But the kids still were not sure. "Put your feet on the windowsill," they yelled. And the wolf put both his white, floured feet up for them to see.

With the sweet voice and the white feet, the kids decided it must be their mother this time, so they opened the door. The wolf ran into the room. The kids ran this way and that trying to hide, but he found and ate every one of them whole, except one, whom he did not find hiding under the sink.

When their mother returned home and found the house in a complete mess, she wept. The tables were overturned, the covers were ripped from the bed, and the curtains were torn down from the windows. "Oh, no!" cried the mother goat. "My poor children."

And she went through the house calling each of them by name. When she came to the one kid's name, he answered! "Mother, here I am." She ran to him and kissed him from head to toe while he told the awful story.

Mother Goat and her only child left the house to go for a walk. They hadn't gone far when they came upon the wolf who was fast asleep on his back. They stood and watched in amazement while the wolf's stomach jumped this way and that! "Could it be that he swallowed them all whole?" wondered the mother. She ran back to the house and got her scissors and thread. Then she cut the wolf open while he slept soundly. All six kids jumped out of the hole and smiled quietly while their mother put a finger to her lips, motioning for them to be quiet. Then she quickly stuffed some rocks into the wolf's stomach and sewed him back up! Mother Goat and the seven little kids danced around merrily in the bushes, laughing.

At last the wolf woke. The rocks in his stomach were very heavy and made him very thirsty. He stumbled along to the river with Mother Goat and her seven kids quietly following behind him. At last he reached the river. When he leaned over to get a drink, the rocks in his stomach made him tumble right down into the water and he sank to the bottom! Never again would the Mother Goat and her seven little kids have to be frightened of the wolf!

The End

MR. AND MRS. HEDGEHOG AND THE HARE (62)

Mr. Hare was a rabbit and spent lots of time playing jokes on Mr. Hedgehog. Mr. Hare teased Mr. Hedgehog about how much faster he could run. Mr. Hedgehog had finally landed on a plan that would really work. He went to Mr. Hare and challenged him. "Tomorrow morning in the cabbage patch, you and I will race, and I will beat you this time!" bragged Mr. Hedgehog.

They met the next morning. Mr. Hare laughed and again said nobody could possibly beat him. "I'm the fastest runner around these parts," he laughed. "Not today. You get ready to be beat. Our lanes will be these cabbages. You stay on this side, and I'll stay on that side. We'll run straight down the row and first one to the end wins," said Mr. Hedgehog. They squatted down and counted, "One, two, three, go!" Mr. Hare ran fast, but when he got to the end of the row of cabbages, there stood a hedgehog!

"Oh, I wasn't really trying. Let's do it again," said Mr. Hare. "One, two, three, go!" he yelled, and Mr. Hare ran really fast, but when he got to the end of the row, there stood a hedgehog! "Oh, this is dumb, I know I can beat you. Let's do it again," begged Mr. Hare. "One, two, three, go!" he yelled, and Mr. Hare ran as fast as his legs would go, but when he got to the end of the row, there stood a hedgehog. "Once more, please," begged the rabbit, but again he got to the end of the row and there stood a smiling hedgehog.

Now Mr. Hare was panting and gasping for breath, but Mr. Hedgehog stood there all calm and cool. He wasn't even breathing hard. "Well, Mr. Smarty Hare, are you ready to give up yet?" asked Mr. Hedgehog. "No, just one more time and I know I'll beat you, now that I'm all warmed up," cried Mr. Hare. Now this time, that rabbit ran so fast you could hardly see him, but when he got to the end of the row, there stood a hedgehog! "Now I give up," gasped Mr. Hare. "I'll never tease you again about me running faster than you," he said. And he walked off very slowly. He was so tired!

Now as soon as he was gone, Mr. Hedgehog rolled all over the ground laughing. His wife was at the other end of the row and she, too, was rolling on the ground laughing! They had neither one ever moved from their spot and were neither one out of breath! They just stuck their heads up each time Mr. Hare got to the end of a row of cabbages. They had finally played a joke on Mr. Hare and he wouldn't be teasing them again about what slow hedgehogs they were!

The End

PETER PAN (3)

A long time ago Wendy, John and Michael Darling lived in a small house, just like you and me. They had a wonderful watchdog dog named "Nana" who would never let the children come to any harm. Nana would lie outside the door while Mrs. Darling told her children fairy stories as she put them to bed.

One night, Mrs. Darling watched her children drop off to sleep and then she dropped off into a bit of a snooze herself. Suddenly she was awakened by a small boy and a bright little light flittering about the room. Had it been a natural little boy like John or Michael, she would not have been frightened, but this little boy was actually flying about the room! Mrs. Darling screamed and Nana ran in. Nana was not afraid of the boy or the light and barked and chased them around. The boy and the light were too fast and were soon out the window, but not quite quickly enough. Nana had caught the boy's shadow with her teeth! Mrs. Darling had no idea what to do with it, so she rolled it up and laid it on the dresser. My, that was an odd thing to happen!

The next night the Darlings were dressing to go out when Nana brushed up against Mr. Darling's new pants and got hair all over them. Mr. Darling was angry and he sent Nana outside. When they left for the party, no one was in the house with the children except their babysitter who was downstairs.

Suddenly the strange little boy flew into the children's room. A little fairy flew beside him and was flickering like a light! The boy was hunting for his shadow. The little fairy found the shadow and tried to get it back on the boy, but they did not know how to stick it on! The noises they made wakened all three children. The children were not frightened, but only watched with curiosity.

"Hi! I'm Peter Pan and this is Tinkerbell," said the boy. He told them how he had lost his shadow but now could not get it back on. So Wendy hopped out of her bed, grabbed her little sewing kit and began to sew the shadow back on to Peter's shoes while he told the children about his home.

"I live in Never Land. I have lived there ever since I ran away from home when I was a boy. I heard my parents talking about how I would one day grow up and become a man. I do not intend to ever grow up and be a man! That is not the life for me! In Never Land children do not grow up, but remain children forever. We live and play with the fairies, like Tinkerbell! Sometimes we even kill pirates!"

Wendy asked him where his mother was now. "Oh, I have no mother. None of us do. The only thing mothers are good for is telling stories, and that is why I came here, to listen to your mother telling stories to you so that I could go back to Never Land and tell some good stories to the other boys who live with me.

But Wendy insisted that all children needed mothers to mend their clothes and fix their meals, not just to tell them stories. Peter thought she might have a good idea at that, and invited Wendy to come to Never Land and be their pretend mother. He promised them such fun and told them he could teach them to fly. Fly? "Oh yes, please take us!" they all shouted.

It was a long way to Never Land. They floated on the clouds and swung on the moon and the stars. They had a great time. At last they arrived in Never Land. Peter told the boys Wendy was to be their new mother but they were surprised. "A mother for us?" They were not so sure they wanted a mother anymore. Soon though they were glad because Wendy tucked them into their beds at night and told them all kinds of wonderful stories. They tried to act unhappy about going to bed, they really could hardly wait each night for bed and story time.

The bad part about Never Land was the pirates. Captain Hook was their leader. He was always on the prowl to find Peter and wanted to kill him. Many years ago Peter had cut off one of Hook's hands and thrown it to a crocodile. Now the Captain only had a metal hook instead of his hand. The crocodile always swam nearby, waiting for another chance to eat Captain Hook's other tasty hand! But Captain Hook always had a warning of the crocodile when it got too close, for once the crocodile had swallowed a clock and the clock still ticked inside the crocodile. He worried the clock would one day run down and might quit ticking!

Captain Hook was a miserable and mean man. When he found out that Peter and the boys had Wendy as their new mother, he became jealous and wanted Wendy to come and be his mother. Then one day while Peter was gone the pirates captured Wendy and the boys and took them to their ship. They begged Wendy to be their mother, but she said she would never be the mother of such bad men. So the men tied her up and said they would make all the boys walk the plank!

Wendy and the boys did not need to be frightened for long, for Tinkerbell had seen the pirates take Wendy and the boys and had flown to tell Peter. It wasn't long before Peter and Tinkerbell boarded the ship to fight for the boys and Wendy.

It was easy for Peter to get aboard. He pretended to be the crocodile by making ticking sounds. The ticking sounds made Captain Hook run and hide. While he was hiding, Peter untied the boys. When Captain Hook finally came out from his hiding spot, they had a great fight! The boys were small enough that they would run between the pirates' legs and the pirates either cut themselves or fell overboard just trying to catch them!

At last none of the pirates were left except Captain Hook himself. He fought with Peter a long time until at last he was too tired to fight any longer. Not hearing the crocodile ticking (for as he feared, at last the clock had run down and stopped ticking), Captain Hook jumped into the water to rest, but the hungry crocodile was there and finished old Hook off with just three bites!

Wendy and her brothers were missing their parents by now. They talked about their home and their mother and all the stories she told them. Wendy soon talked her brothers and even all the other boys, except Peter, into going home with her. But Peter did not want to go back there and grow up. He did guide them all back to Wendy's home, but Peter left them all there and flew back to Never Land.

Mr. and Mrs. Darling were so excited to see their children again and hugged them so hard they could barely breathe! They welcomed all the boys and agreed to adopt each and every one of them.

As for Peter, he still lives in Never Land. Once a year he visits Wendy who is now a grown woman with a daughter of her own. And once a year, Wendy's daughter goes with Peter for a week to visit Never Land and tell stories to the new boys that live there with Peter now.

The End

PETER RABBIT (77)

Peter was a little boy bunny rabbit. He lived with his mother and three sisters, Flopsy, Mopsy, and Cottontail in a hole in the ground. Peter played with his sisters, but they were not as daring as he, and he often went in search of more adventure than his sisters wanted to get into.

One day Peter's mother was baking bread. "Now children, all of you run out and play so I can get my baking done. Don't wander off too far, and be sure not to go to Farmer McGregor's. That is a bad and dangerous place for bunny rabbits to go," she warned.

Flopsy, Mopsy and Cottontail took a jumping rope outside and began to jump the rope. "Come on Peter, jump with us," they called. But Peter shook his head, "I'm going to find adventure. Come with me," be begged. But they would not go, so he went alone.

Peter hopped down the road for a time and then he spied Mr. McGregor's garden. Oh, everything smelled so good! He knew he shouldn't go into this garden, but he only wanted a nibble. He squirmed under the fence and ran straight for the carrots. He pulled up one carrot and ate it. It tasted so good that he had to have another. He ate that one, too, and then he saw the lettuce. "My, that looks good," he mumbled to himself. He hopped over and nibbled at the lettuce for a while. Then he just had to have a radish and he ran over to them. But as he sat there nibbling on a radish he heard footsteps and there stood Mr. McGregor himself! "What do you think you're doing eating my radishes?" yelled Mr. McGregor.

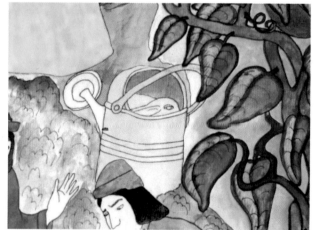

Well, Peter was off like a shot! He ran, but Mr. McGregor was right on his tail! Then Peter saw the strawberry patch and ran for it. He lost one of his shoes there, so he kicked off the other. Now he could really run! Without shoes, he was much faster than Mr. McGregor and soon lost him. Peter hid in the strawberry patch until Mr. McGregor gave up and went back to his work.

Peter thought he better be getting back home and started off in the direction he had come from. But as he came to the cabbages, he had to stop. Oh did they smell good! So he sat there and nibbled at the cabbages for a time. My, he was really getting full! He knew he would have to go soon because Mother might be looking for him by now.

Suddenly, there stood Mr. McGregor again. "Oh, no!" yelled Peter and off he ran. He ran this way and that dodging from Mr. McGregor. If he only hadn't ate so much he might be able to run faster. Then Mr. McGregor stumbled and fell down. He wasn't down long, but it was long enough for Peter to get away. Peter shook off his little jacket and ran for the shed. He found a watering can and jumped into it. Splash! Peter hadn't known there would be water in the can!

Peter sat there in the can of water for a long time it seemed before he began to sneeze. Mr. McGregor had been turning over everything in the shed trying to find Peter, but when he heard that sneeze, he grabbed the watering can. He shook that watering can until Peter fell out, but he just didn't grab him fast enough. By now, Peter was so scared that he could outrun anyone! He ran as fast as his little legs would carry him. He scrambled under the fence and ran for home, escaping from Mr. McGregor!

When Peter stumbled into his little home, his mother scolded him. "Peter, where are your jacket and shoes? And why are you all wet?" she asked. But Peter couldn't do anything except stand there and sneeze and hold onto his full, sick stomach. Peter's mother had to give him a big dose of medicine and put him to bed, while Flopsy, Mopsy and Cottontail had fresh baked bread for their supper.

The End

PINOCCHIO (no number for this story because although he is painted on the fairy tale print, hanging from the grandmother's rocking chair, he mistakenly did not make it into the Legend which told where the various stories were drawn on the mural)

There once was a toy maker named Geppetto who carved wooden puppets. He wanted so much to have a little boy of his own to love so one day he carved a little boy puppet and named him Pinocchio. Geppetto wished Pinocchio was real, but he was only made of wood. One night while he was sleeping a blue fairy appeared to Geppetto. She granted part of his wish for Pinocchio to walk and talk, but she left him wooden. She told Pinocchio he must be good and earn the right to be a real little boy instead of a wooden boy. She also said if he was not a good boy or told any lies, his nose would grow!

Pinocchio had a hard time being "good" and had a harder time telling the truth about pretty much anything. He thought a little fib was not the same thing as a lie, but when he even told a tiny little fib, his nose grew longer! "Are you lying about that?" Geppetto would ask him and Pinocchio would fib a little bit again and say, "No, it's the truth!" and his nose would grow a little longer again!

At school his teacher would ask where his homework was and he would often lie and say his dog ate it, and again his nose would grow longer! One time he ran off and joined a circus, but he told so many lies and his nose got so long that they kicked him out and he went back home. Pretty soon his nose was so long he had a hard time walking straight and not tipping over!

Although Geppetto told Pinocchio to always come straight home from school, Pinocchio often took small detours through places he wanted to play instead of going straight home. Sometimes he stopped by the ocean but when Geppetto told him, "Do NOT go the ocean alone!" Pinocchio would shake his head and lie again, "Oh, no! I will come straight home from school," and his nose grew a bit longer!

One day Pinocchio was so late that Geppetto was worried and went looking for him. He called out, "Pinocchio! Pinocchio! Where are you?" No answer. Geppetto was getting upset and went down by the ocean to see if Pinocchio went there again instead of going home like he was supposed to. He went out to the edge of the wharf and yelled again, "Pinocchio! Pinocchio!" but still no answer.

Just then the boards on the wharf gave way and Geppetto went KERSPLASH and fell right into the ocean! Geppetto splashed and flopped around. A big old whale spotted all the splashing, swam up and swallowed Geppetto! Oh no! Inside the whale's tummy Geppetto swam around! "How do I get out of here?" he yelled, but nobody else could hear him.

Pinocchio burst into the house that afternoon, late as usual. But Geppetto was nowhere to be found. Pinocchio went outside and called for him, but Geppetto did not answer. A neighbor said he saw Geppetto going down to the ocean. "Why would he go there? Oh-oh! I bet he was trying to find me," exclaimed Pinocchio, and he raced down to the ocean, just in time to see Geppetto falling off the wharf and being swallowed by the whale!

Pinocchio jumped into the water and swam straight for the whale! He knocked and knocked on the whale's jaw until the startled whale opened his mouth in surprise! Pinocchio was able to swim inside where he found Geppetto splashing around. Geppetto was so glad to see Pinocchio and hugged him tightly, but now they were both trapped!

"Let's tickle his cheeks and make him laugh," said Pinocchio. Geppetto thought that a stupid idea, but he didn't have any other ideas himself, so they both started tickling the whale's cheeks! Tickle..tickle..tickle! It worked! The whale started giggling, and then he laughed right out loud and Geppetto and Pinocchio were both able to swim out and over to the shore. "Whew! That was scary," said Pinocchio. "Thanks for saving my life," said Geppetto, and he hugged Pinocchio tightly.

That night, while they were sleeping, the blue fairy came to Geppetto again. She had been watching over Pinocchio all the time and now she saw that he had feelings just like any other little boy! She granted Geppetto's wish that Pinocchio not be just a wooden toy any more, but a real live son. When they woke up, Pinocchio was no longer made of wood and no longer had a long pointy noise. He was now a real live boy, just like you and me!

The End

PUSS IN BOOTS (22)

When the old miller died he left only one thing for his young son, a cat named Puss. Now, the young son was upset at losing his father, but to be left only with a cat, how was he to make his living?

"Do not fear," said the cat. "Buy me a jacket, a green hat, a bag, and a pair of fine red boots and I will make you rich!" The young man could not see how Puss could make him rich but went ahead and bought the new clothes. Then the young man decided that just Puss was too plain a name and renamed his cat Puss In Boots.

The next day Puss In Boots took his new bag out into the fields and stuffed it full of carrots. Then he hid in the bushes. Along came a rabbit and went into the bag to get the carrots. Puss In Boots snatched up the bag and pulled the string shut. He took the rabbit to the king. "Oh, gracious King, I have brought you a gift from the Marquis of Carabas," he said. Well, the king was not about to let anyone know that he had never heard of such an important sounding person, so merely said, "Thank him for me." Actually there was no real Marquis of Carabas, but Puss In Boots had a plan!

The next day Puss In Boots stuffed his bag, with grain, caught a turkey and took it to the Kings servants. He told the servants that these were gifts were from the Marquis of Carabas and to give them to the king.

Puss In Boots waited around the castle until he heard that the king and his daughter were going for a ride by the river and maybe on to the magician's castle. He ran to his master and told him to go and swim in the river. The young man did not understand, but why not go swimming anyway? The young man pulled off his clothes and jumped into the river. Puss In Boots hid his master's clothes and when he saw the king coming he ran to the carriage and yelled, "Help, help! The Marquis of Carabas is drowning!" The king's servants jumped in and pulled him out of the river and saw that he was naked. "Some robbers stole his clothes and threw him into the river!" yelled Puss In Boots. So, the king ordered his servants to run back and get clothing fit for such a noble person as the Marquis of Carabas. When he put the clothes on he looked so handsome that the princess fell in love with him at first sight and he, too, fell in love with her.

The princes and the king then returned to their journey. The king asked the young man to go with them and he climbed into their carriage. Puss In Boots ran down the road ahead of them. He came to a field where gardeners were working. "The king is coming! When he asks who these fields belong to, you be sure to answer 'The Marquis of Carabas' or your heads will be mine!" When the king came through the fields he was told the owner's name before he could even ask!

Puss In Boots ran on to the castle of the great wicked magician. "Oh, great magician, I have heard such wonders about you that I had to come see for myself how great you really are," cried Puss In Boots. 'Well," said the magician, "you heard correctly. I am the greatest magician." "Can you make yourself into something as big as a lion," asked Puss in Boots? "Of course I can," and he turned himself into a lion. When he was himself again, Puss In Boots asked if he could make himself as small as a mouse, and showing off, the magician turned into a mouse. Quick as a wink, Puss In Boots gobbled up the mouse!

Puss In Boots ran to the door as his master and the king arrived. "Welcome to the home of the Marquis of Carabas," said Puss In Boots. The servants were so glad to be rid of the wicked magician that they welcomed this new master and fixed a fine feast. During the feast the new Lord of his new castle asked the princess to marry him, and she said she would. So, Puss In Boots did indeed make his master rich!

The End

RAPUNZEL (1)

A long time ago there lived a man and woman who wanted a child very badly. One day the woman was looking out her window into the garden of the witch who lived next door. The garden was full of lettuce and the woman wanted to run out and pick the lettuce so badly she could almost taste it. Nothing would satisfy her but the lettuce in the witch's garden. Her husband worried about his wife for she became very weak. Even though they had no money to spare, the man knew he had to get the lettuce for his wife. Better to steal the lettuce than to let his wife die of hunger.

That night he jumped over the fence and picked some lettuce. His wife was so happy and she gobbled up the lettuce as quickly as could be. The next day she wanted the lettuce again and refused to eat anything else. Her husband decided he would go to the witch's garden again but as he was picking the lettuce, the old witch ran out screaming, "Stop, you thief! How dare you steal my lettuce! Now you shall die!" The man was frightened, but stood quietly and tried to explain how badly his wife wanted the lettuce. The witch listened carefully and then said, I will let you go now, but when your first child is born, you must give it to me." He did not think they would ever have a child anyway, so he thoughtlessly promised her what she asked. But shortly thereafter, a child was born to them and the witch came to claim the child. She named her Rapunzel.

Rapunzel grew into the most beautiful girl in the land. The witch was so jealous of Rapunzel's beauty that she locked Rapunzel in a high tower that had no stairway or door, but only a small window at the top. When the witch came to feed Rapunzel she called out from below, "Rapunzel, Rapunzel, let down your hair." Rapunzel had such long and lovely golden hair that she would let it out the window and the witch would climb up the braids of her hair.

Rapunzel was a sad and lonely girl in the high tower and often sang to herself to pass the time. One day as she was singing a prince rode by. Her voice was so sweet. He had to find out who was singing. He circled round and round the tower but could find no entrance. He sat down behind some trees to think about how to get in. Just then the old witch came and called out "Rapunzel, Rapunzel, let down your hair!" Rapunzel let her braids down the tall tower and the witch climbed up. The prince was happy to see how he could get up to the sweet voice. When the witch left, the prince called to Rapunzel and she let down her hair thinking it was the witch again. But when she saw the prince she was frightened. She had never seen a man before. The prince fell in love with the beautiful girl at once. "You are so beautiful and lonely. Leave this tower and come be my wife." he begged.

Rapunzel thought it would be better to marry this nice man than live with the witch who kept her locked up and so she agreed to marry him. "But I cannot get down," she said. "Each time you come to see me, bring some twine. I will braid it and one day it will be long and strong enough that I can climb down," she said.

The prince came to see Rapunzel each evening since the witch came during the day. But one day, thoughtlessly, Rapunzel said to the witch, "How is it you are so slow to climb when the prince climbs up so quickly?" The witch was enraged. "So you have been sneaking behind my back?" she screamed at Rapunzel. She cut off Rapunzel's hair with two snips of her scissors and took her into the desert to wander alone.

That evening the prince came to see Rapunzel. He climbed the braids the witch had hooked to a peg in the tower. When he reached the top, there stood the witch! He jumped out the window in fear for his life. He was not killed, but in the fall he was blinded. He stumbled off, unable to see, and walked for miles. He stumbled blindly through the woods. He could see nothing. And then he stopped. Did he hear someone singing! He did! He knew it was Rapunzel's voice because only she could sing so sweetly. He stumbled toward the sweet voice. Rapunzel saw him and ran to him weeping and when her tears touched his eyes, his eyes were healed and he could see her beautiful face again. The prince took Rapunzel back to his castle and they were married and lived happily ever after.

The End

RUMPLESTILTSKIN (37)

Many years ago a miller told a wicked king that he had a daughter that was so clever she could spin straw into gold. "Send her to me tomorrow so I may admire her," said the king. The next day the miller's daughter appeared before the wicked king. The king took her into a room full of straw and told her to spin it into gold before morning or she would lose her life. He left, locking the door behind him.

The poor girl sat in the room and cried. She had no idea how to spin straw into gold. Why had her father told such a lie? What would she do? Presently the door opened and a little strange man came in and asked why she was crying. "The king says I must spin this straw into gold or I shall die. I have no idea how to do such a thing," cried the girl. So the man offered to do it for her if she would only give him her necklace. She agreed at once and handed him her necklace.

The little man sat at the spinning wheel and in no time had spun all the straw into gold. It was so easy for him for he was a magician. The next morning he was gone before the king came. The king was amazed to see the room full of gold and not straw. So he took the girl to a larger room with even more straw. He ordered her to spin it into gold or she would still die.

Again the poor girl was crying when the little man came in. This time he offered to spin the straw into gold if she would give him her ring. She agreed at once and the little man soon was busily spinning the gold. When the king came the next morning the man was gone. The king thought the girl truly a blessed maiden and he took the girl to another room. It was larger than both the others had been and had lots more straw. "Spin this straw into gold and I will make you my wife. If not, you will die," he threatened.

When the little man came in the girl wept bitterly. "I have nothing left to give you," cried the girl. "Promise me that when you become queen you will give me your first child, and I will do it for you," said the man. The girl had no choice. She would die if the gold was not spun and so she agreed. The king was delighted the next morning and at once made the girl his wife.

Some time later the girl, now a queen, had a child. She was sitting quietly with her child one evening when the little man came to her. "Remember your promise to give me the child?" he asked. But the queen wept so bitterly that he felt sorry for her. "If you can guess my name within three days, you can keep the child," he said.

The queen spent the next day trying to guess what his name could be. He had only told her that was a very unusual name. When he came to her that evening she asked, "Is your name Crastin, or Boblink or Dingledorf?" but he only said, "No," to each name she spoke.

On the second day the queen had asked all the names in the town. She asked him that evening, "Is your name Bathbora, or Ocean or Shacambie?" and all sorts of other odd names, but he always replied, "No."

On the third day the queen sent a messenger out to ask strange names of people all over the land. The messenger came back just before the man was to arrive. "I have some more names but the oddest I heard was when I saw a little man dancing around a tree. He was singing, "This evening a baby I will hold, for spinning straw into gold. The queen - she is not to blame for not knowing Rumplestiltskin is my name!"

When the little man came to the queen she said, "Is your name Coulter, or Kimarand or Roxanne?" To each he replied "No." The queen looked at him quietly and then asked, "Well, then, is it Rumplestiltskin?"

The little man went into a rage. "How could you know? How could you guess?" He got so mad that he stomped his feet so hard that he squashed himself into a flat golden coin.

The End

SLEEPING BEAUTY (38)

A baby girl had been born to the king and queen! Everyone in the land rejoiced! The king and queen invited all the fairies of the land to come to the child's christening, for it was the custom that the fairies all bestowed a gift of love and happiness to babies.

The day of the christening, seven fairies came together. They had not been there long before an eighth fairy arrived. "Why was I not invited?" she demanded. The king answered that all the fairies were invited and she must not have gotten his message. But that did not convince the wicked fairy and she decided to do harm to this child, but the youngest fairy read her mind. When it was time to bestow their gifts, the youngest fairy hid herself so she would be last. The first six fairies bestowed things such as the child would be the prettiest in the land, she would be the sweetest singer in the land, and the like. Then the eighth wicked fairy came and put a curse on the child that before she was sixteen she would prick her finger on a spindle and die.

"I cannot completely undo what the wicked fairy has cursed, but I can help," said the youngest fairy as she came out from her hiding spot. She went to the child and bestowed her gift. "Yes, you will prick your finger, but you will not die. You and all the

people in the castle will go to sleep for one hundred years. Then a prince will find you and kiss you and you will waken." The king was horrified at all this. Just to be safe, he had all the spindles in the land collected and burned, hoping to stop the curse.

Over the years the baby grew to be a beautiful girl. As the fairies predicted, she really was the prettiest girl in the land and could sing the sweetest. Now, nearing her sixteenth birthday, preparations were made for a big birthday party! The king and queen were very busy and did not notice when their daughter went wandering about alone. The castle was so big that the girl was always finding new spots she had not seen before. Today she found a door at the top of a stairway. She went in and there sat an old lady at a spinning wheel. "What is that?" asked the girl, for she had never seen a spinning wheel.

Now the old lady was not just any old lady, she was really the wicked eighth fairy who had put the curse on her at the christening party. "Come here and I'll show you how to work it," said the old lady. The girl went to the wheel and as soon as she touched it, she pricked her finger. She fell to the floor, asleep instantly. Suddenly all the servants, the maids and even the dogs started falling asleep. The king realized what was happening and ran to find his daughter sleeping on the floor. He picked her up and carried her to her own bed. Then he, too, fell asleep.

One hundred years went by and the castle and everything in it slept. The trees and vines grew over it so thick it was nearly covered. One day a prince was out riding and came upon the castle. He found people sleeping everywhere. He wandered around all through the castle and eventually he came upon the sleeping princess. She was so beautiful that he could not help bending to kiss her. As he kissed her, she awoke! "You must be the prince I have been dreaming about for so long," she whispered sleepily.

Then all around the castle, the people and animals awoke. The king ran to his daughter's room and found her talking with the prince. The prince and princess soon fell in love and made preparations to be married. They made the most beautiful couple, and when the king and queen grew old and died, the prince and princess became the new king and queen, and of course, they lived happily ever after.

The End

SNOW WHITE AND ROSE RED (80)

Many years ago a woman lived with her two daughters in the forest. The two daughters were named Snow White and Rose Red. They were good little girls and helped their mother keep the house as neat as a pin. They played in the forest with the animals in the summer when they finished with their work, but during the winter they stayed in the house for it was very cold.

One winter night there was a knock at the door. Rose Red opened the door and there stood a big bear! "Please let me come in and sit by your fire so I may warm myself," begged the bear. The bear seemed friendly enough so they brushed the snow from his back and led him in to the fire. The bear slept there soundly all night. He spent the rest of the winter leaving during the daytime, and returning each night to sleep by the fire. The girls loved the bear and they became good friends. When spring came the bear said he would have to leave now and live like all bears do, but he would return the next winter. And he did. For many years, the bear returned and slept there each night during the winter.

One summer day the girls, now young ladies, were walking in the forest. Suddenly they heard a little man yelling for help. He had caught his beard in the bushes.

The girls pulled and pulled, but they could not free the little man's beard. Then Snow White pulled a little pair of scissors from her pocket and cut the beard free. "You stupid girl!" yelled the man. "Why did you cut my beard?" She told him she was only trying to help, but he ran off muttering to himself without even a thank you.

The next day the girls ran across the little man again. He had been fishing and now had caught his beard in the fishing line. The girls pulled and pulled, but they could not free his beard. Again Snow White pulled her scissors out and cut a little bit more of the man's beard so that he was free. "You dimwit! You have cut my beard again!" yelled the man. Rose Red tried to explain there was no other way to free him, but the man ran off into the forest.

Not long after that, the girls came upon the same man again. An eagle had dived down and was pulling at the man's beard. Snow White and Rose Red ran to hold onto the little man and tried to pull him free, but they could not. Finally Snow White pulled her scissors out and cut the remainder of the man's beard completely off! The eagle flew off with the rest of the beard, but the little man stood there dumbfounded. "My poor magic beard. You have cut it completely off! What shall I do now?" moaned the man.

At that moment a handsome prince came up to them. "Hello Snow White and Rose Red," said the prince. "How do you know us?" asked the girls. "I am the bear that lives with you each winter. This little man put a curse on me many years ago and changed me into a bear. Now that his magic beard is gone, I am free to be myself again," said the prince. He told Snow White that he had grown to love her over the years and he wanted her to come and be his bride and she agreed at once.

The two girls and the prince went to get the girls' mother and they all went to the castle to unite the prince with his family again. His father and brother were delighted with his story. It wasn't long before his brother fell in love with Rose Red. She was so beautiful, just like Snow White. And the prince's brother was as handsome as the prince. Snow White and the prince, and Rose Red and the prince's brother were married in one big happy wedding and they all lived happily ever after.

The End

SNOW WHITE AND THE SEVEN DWARFS (56)

Once upon a time a baby girl was born to a queen and king. They named her Snow White. The queen and king were happy with their new child, but sadly, the queen died soon after Snow White was born. The king did not want his daughter to grow up without a mother, and in time, the king married again. The new queen was very beautiful and vain and she had a magic mirror. She would ask the mirror, "Mirror, Mirror, on the wall, who is the most beautiful of all?" and it would always reply that she was.

Over the years, Snow White began to grow into a pretty girl. The queen was jealous and could not stand Snow White being so pretty. The new queen made Snow White work in the kitchen and scrub all the floors, but this did not stop Snow White from becoming more beautiful every day. Snow White grew older and more beautiful as the years went by. One day when the queen asked her magic mirror, "Mirror, Mirror on the wall, who is the most beautiful of them all?" the mirror answered, "Snow White is the most beautiful of them all!"

Horrified to hear the mirror's opinion, the queen called a servant to her and said, "Take Snow White into the forest and kill her. To be sure you do, bring back her heart to me." The servant tried to argue with the queen that he could not bear to kill the lovely girl, but the queen said he would die if he did not do as she said. So the servant led Snow White into the forest. He told her what he was supposed to do, but could not. "Run into the forest and hide. Never let the queen know you are alive," he said sadly. Then he killed a goat and took the goat's heart to the queen. The queen was satisfied the girl was dead and did not bother to talk with her mirror for a time.

Snow White ran into the forest as the servant told her. She walked a long way and became very tired. At last she came upon a tiny house. She knocked at the door, but no one was home. "Surely they would not mind if I went in and rested," she thought. She walked into the little house and saw seven little beds. The beds were so tiny that she lie down across all seven beds and fell asleep.

That evening seven tiny men, called dwarfs, returned home and found the beautiful girl sleeping on their beds. They were so entranced with her beauty they did not have the heart to waken her, so they all lay down on the floor and went to sleep for the night.

The next morning when Snow White woke, there stood the seven little dwarfs. The dwarfs were so small and unusual that she was frightened at first. "Don't be afraid of us but please tell us why you are here," asked one of the little men, and Snow White told them her story.

The seven little dwarfs huddled together for a few moments and mumbled. Then one spoke up. "Snow White, you could live here with us. Why don't you stay and be our mother?" She agreed, for she liked these seven unusual little men at once. Such merry, sweet men they were. They told her not to let anyone in the house, for the queen might one day find out that she was still alive and try to harm her. Then they marched off to work, singing "hi ho, hi ho, it's off to work we go!"

Time went by happily for Snow White. She loved living with the dwarfs. They were so good to her. She cooked and cleaned and sewed for them as though they were her own children. But one day the wicked queen went to her mirror again. When she asked who was the most beautiful in the land, it answered that Snow White was the most beautiful in the land and told the queen where to find her. The queen became very angry. She would not trust a servant this time. She disguised herself as a beggar woman, put poison into an apple, gathered up some more apples and started off to find Snow White.

When she reached the house, Snow White came to the door. "I'm selling apples for my living. Could you buy some from me?" asked the wicked queen. She was disguised so well that Snow White did not recognize her, yet she did not let the woman into the house. "I cannot afford to buy any apples, dear lady, but perhaps another time I can," answered Snow White sweetly. The wicked queen pretended to feel sorry for the girl and handed Snow White the poisoned apple. "You eat this one then, just for yourself," said the queen and went away. Snow White stood there with the apple and tried to think how to split it with the seven little men, but she knew it would never work. Finally she decided to call it her supper and she bit into the apple. As she did, she fell to the floor as though she were dead!

When the seven dwarfs came home that night they found Snow White on the floor. They did everything they could to revive her. They knew she was not dead, for she still breathed, but still she would not waken. Finally, they built her a little glass bed and placed it in the forest. Six of the dwarfs went off to work each day, but they always took turns leaving one of the dwarfs to stay and watch over the pretty Snow White sleeping on the glass bed.

One day a prince came riding by. "Who is this beautiful sleeping girl?" he asked the dwarf that was watching over her that day. The dwarf told him the story. "Oh, she is so beautiful! May I kiss her just once?" asked the prince. The dwarf could see no harm in the kiss and lifted the glass lid so the prince might kiss her. As he kissed Snow White she awakened! She sat up and asked why she was sleeping in the woods. The prince told her the story and said he was already in love with her. Would she come live in his castle with him and be his bride? She answered at once that she would be his bride. The prince lifted her onto his horse and told the dwarf to bring the other six little men and come to the wedding the next day.

That very day, the wicked queen went to her magic mirror. She asked who was the most beautiful in the land and when it answered that Snow White was the most beautiful and was even being married that day, the queen went into such a rage that she died!

After the wedding was performed, the prince asked the seven dwarfs to move into the castle with them. And the prince, the seven little dwarfs and Snow White lived happily ever after.

The End

THE BEAR AND THE BEES, A FABLE (8)

One day a bear happened to come upon a beehive. Thinking the honey from the hive might make a good meal, he stopped to see what he could do about getting some of the honey out of the hive.

The bear had only been poking about for a moment when one of the bees came home. The bee, seeing the bear and knowing what he was up to promptly stung the bear on the nose and flew inside the beehive.

The bear was enraged! "Sting me, will you? Well, I'll show you!" he cried, and he pounced upon the beehive! But he had no sooner than pounced upon it when two hundred and sixty-eight bees came swarming out upon him. The bear had to run for his life!

Running away, the bear realized he should have left with only one sting than to be a bully and end up with two hundred and sixty-eight more stings!

The End

Moral: Don't let your anger make things worse

THE BIG BALLOON (2)

My grandmother told of a time when she was a small child. She lived in a very small town with only a few houses, one church, one schoolhouse and one store. One day a tall man came to town and went through the town yelling, "Come take a ride in the big balloon! Come ride the big balloon for only a nickel." All the people came running out of their houses to see what was going on.

In this town there lived three little children, Katie, who was seven, Harry, her brother, who was five, and their little sister, May, who was three. They looked at the big balloon with big eyes and their mouths gaped open very wide! "How does it work?" they asked the tall man. He explained how the balloon was filled with helium gas which made it rise into the air and float. The only reason it was on the ground now was because he had it tied down to a stake with a strong rope. The children were delighted with the idea of the balloon and begged their parents to let them take a ride. "Why not?" said the father and paid the tall man.

The three children climbed into the basket under the balloon. The tall man stood below and slowly unwound the rope to let the balloon rise higher and higher. Suddenly a little dog jumped on the man and knocked him down and as he fell, he let go of the rope! He ran after the rope, but the balloon rose so fast he could not catch it. All the other people who were just watching were now running after the rope but no one could

catch it! Higher and higher the big balloon went! There was nothing the tall man or anybody else could do to bring it back.

The children floated off into the air, high above the clouds! Katie, Harry and May were having a great time! They didn't know the tall man now didn't know how to bring them back down. The children watched the people and the houses get smaller and smaller until at last they had disappeared completely. They watched the clouds and birds float gracefully by. They spent the rest of the day amazed at all the beauty. They even saw a rainbow!

Toward evening Harry said, "I'm hungry. Let's go back home now," and Little May agreed. They looked around the basket but could find nothing that would make it go down! "What do we do now?" asked Harry. As their older sister Katie had no answer for them, they went on talking about how hungry they were. Little May smiled and said, "I have three crackers in my pocket!" She pulled them out and handed one to Katie and one to Harry and ate the last one herself.

Harry, usually not afraid of anything, thought about all the bad places they might drift down upon. "What if we float right onto a train and it carries us a long way off? Or what if we land on a church steeple? How would we ever get down?" But Katie, being oldest, acted bravely for her little brother and sister and assured them that the big balloon would eventually land and they would all be safe.

In time it began to get dark. At first the children were scared, but then the moon came out and shined so brightly that it seemed almost light in the little basket under the big balloon. Harry brightened up and began to sing a little song:

> "Up around the moon, boys, Sailing round the moon,
> Up around the moon, boys,   Sailing round the moon!"

But Katie hushed him. "Be quiet Harry. We may be near Heaven's gate and we don't want to wake the angels!" But Harry kept right on singing until he had sung himself and little May to sleep.

Katie looked at her little brother and sister laying there sound asleep. How would they get down? Would they ever get down? What were her parents doing now? Now that the two younger ones were asleep, Katie no longer had to pretend to be brave. She started crying very softly until she cried herself to sleep.

Back in the little town the children's parents were so worried. The neighbors brought food for their supper but they were too worried about their children to eat anything. They did not go to bed for they knew they would not be able to sleep. How could they get their children back home?

The next morning when Katie woke, the sun was shining brightly! She wondered if perhaps they had drifted down closer to home by now and she peered over the side of the big basket, but only the clouds were under the big balloon. She leaned way out and then she saw a rope hanging loose. "I wonder what this rope is for?" And as she pulled on it the balloon suddenly dropped very fast and then slowed up and then was still again. Whew!! That sure scared her! Maybe this was the way to get back down? She pulled on the rope again and whoosh, it dropped very fast and then slowed up and became still again. She was careful not to waken her younger brother and sister for she did not want them to be as scared as she was right now. She jerked on the rope again and again. Each time it dropped, slowed and was still. Jerk, drop and slow. Jerk, drop and slow. At last she could see the tree tops. She jerked a few more times and she began to see tiny houses. It was a small town! It even looked a lot like her own town when she got a little lower.

Then she recognized her own church and her own schoolhouse. And then she even saw her own house!

"Wake up, Harry! Wake up May!" she yelled. "We're almost home now!" she yelled happily. Harry and May both woke, yawned and rubbed their eyes. "Home?" they both asked at once. They leaned way over to look down at their town. "Be careful! Don't fall out!" warned their big sister Katie.

Down below the townspeople were running around like little ants. They had seen the balloon coming down. People were running through the streets yelling to each other "The balloon is coming down! The children are coming home! Yay!"

At last, with one final jerk on the rope, the big balloon settled to the ground. The tall man ran to it and grabbed the rope and tied it to the stake. The children's parents pulled them out and kissed and hugged each of them so tight the children could hardly breathe. Yes, they were breathless, but so happy to be back home!

The mayor of the town declared it a holiday and said no children had to go to school that day and he ran to ring the town bell. Then the schoolmaster ran to ring the school bell, the minister ran to ring the church bell and the train engineer ran to ring the train's whistle, toot-toot-toot!

Since that day had been declared a holiday, the whole town had a big celebration. The band played loudly, and someone kept all the bells ringing all day. And to this very day, that little town still celebrates the children's adventure and the return of the big balloon on the same day every year!

The End

THE BOY AND THE NORTH WIND (5)

There was once a boy and his mother who had only a little bit of grain left in the barn. The boy's mother gave him a bowl and told him to go to the barn and fill it with grain. He filled the bowl and on the way back the North Wind came blowing about and blew all the grain from the bowl! The boy went back for more, but on his way back again, the North Wind again blew away all the grain. Now irritated, the boy went back for a third time, and took the last of the grain. He covered the bowl with his hand, but still the North Wind blew through his fingers and blew away the grain! Now upset, the boy told his mother, "I'm going to the North Wind's house and demand he give back our grain!" cried the boy.

The boy walked for two days and at last he came to the house of the North Wind. The North Wind opened the door and the boy said, "You have blown away all our grain and it was the last we had. Please give it back." "I cannot give back your grain for it is scattered here and there, but since you have no food I will give you a magic cloth. Just say, `Cloth, cloth, give me food' and it will feed you," said the North Wind.

Satisfied, the boy left with the cloth. He walked a long time and grew tired. He stopped at a house to ask if he could rest. "Go away. I have no food for you," said the man. "I can provide food for both of us," said the boy. "I just need to rest." He took out the cloth and said, "Cloth, cloth, give me food." Immediately the table was spread with a fine meal and they both sat down and ate to their fill.

When they were full, the man led the boy to a small bed and told him to rest. Now this man was very wicked and when the boy was asleep, the man took the magic cloth and put another plain cloth in its place. The next morning the boy picked up the cloth and went home. He told his mother what the cloth could do and stood back and said the magic words, but the cloth did nothing. "The North Wind has cheated me again. I am going to go back to the North Wind and demand my grain." cried the boy.

He walked the long way back again and angrily yelled at the North Wind. "This cloth is no good! I want my grain back!" demanded the boy.   "I told you the grain is scattered here and there, but I will give you a goat that will produce money if you say: "Goat, goat, make money." The boy agreed and left with the goat.

The boy stopped at the same house where he had stayed before. The man again tried to turn the boy away, but this time the boy said he could pay him with money and the man let him in. The boy said the magic words to the magic goat and out of the goat's mouth tumbled many golden coins. "Oh, thank you," said the wicked old man. "Now you lie down and rest." Again, while the boy was sleeping, the man exchanged the magic goat for a plain goat.

The boy took the goat home to his mother but it could do nothing but stand there and stare at them. No coins came from its mouth no matter what they said. Now, once more, the boy walked back to the North Wind's house.

When he knocked at the North Wind's door again the boy was very angry. "First you blew away my grain three times; then you gave me a cloth that only gave food once and then a goat that only gave money once. I want my grain back!" demanded the boy. "I surely wish I had never blown away your grain, but then I did not know it was your last. I was only having some fun. Take this stick with you and say, "Stick, stick, knock, knock" and it will do anything you want it to. Then say: "Stick, stick, stop, stop" and it will stop," said the North Wind.

The boy started home and the wicked man saw him coming again and went to the door and bid the boy come in. Perhaps the boy would have something magic again, thought the wicked man. The boy hugged the stick to him and lay down and went to sleep.

Although the boy had not mentioned the stick being magic, the man thought it might be with the way the boy kept it so close to him. So after the man thought the boy was asleep, he started for the stick. But the boy was not sleeping for he had figured out by now what might have happened before to his cloth and goat.

"Stick, stick, knock, knock," he yelled. The stick jumped up and ran about the room beating on the man! No way could the man turn or run or hide but the stick was right after him! He yelled for the boy to get the stick off him.   "You stole my magic cloth and my magic goat. If you will give them back, I will make the stick stop!" yelled the boy. "Yes, yes, I will give them back!" yelled the man.

So the boy made the stick stop and collected his magic cloth and magic goat. Then the boy, the stick, the cloth and the goat all went home to his mother.

The End

THE BRAVE LITTLE TAILOR (51)

There was once a young man named Michael who was a tailor. One day while sitting at his table eating bread and jelly, some flies were flying around trying to land on his jelly, so he picked up a towel and killed the flies. When he raised the towel he counted seven dead flies! My, this was really something! Michael grabbed up a piece of leather and immediately went to work making himself a leather badge. He inscribed "Seven With One Blow" on the badge.

The little tailor wore the belt everywhere. His neighbors thought he had killed seven men with one blow, and Michael did not bother telling them different. When the king heard of this he sent for the tailor. The king thought how powerful his army would be to have such a strong and brave man in it.

Before leaving for the palace, the tailor looked through his kitchen for something to eat. He found a piece of cheese, put it in his pocket and headed toward the palace. After walking only a little way he came upon a small bird. The bird did not fly away, so Michael put the bird in his pocket and continued on.

In a little bit he came upon a giant who seemed friendly. The giant, though friendly, loved games. Seeing the belt the giant challenged the tailor, "If you can kill seven with one blow, let us see who is the strongest." Michael did not want to seem afraid and so the contest began.

The giant picked up a rock and squeezed it until the water ran out of it. "Let me see you do that!" he cried. So the tailor picked up a small rock and sneaked the piece of cheese into his hand. He then squeezed his hand into a tight fist and the milk ran out of the cheese.

Then the giant picked up another rock and threw it as hard as he could. Michael pretended to pick up a rock, but then he put the bird in his hand. "Your rock went very far, but when I throw a rock, it never falls to the ground," the tailor said. Then he threw the bird as far as he could. The bird just kept right on flying away.

Then the giant pulled up a tree! "I'll carry the trunk and you carry the branches. We'll see who holds out the longest carrying such a heavy load." The giant picked up the trunk, and Michael hopped up into the branches. The giant could not see him in the branches, so busy he was trying to carry the whole tree. At last the giant gasped, "I cannot hold up my end any longer. Let us put it down." The tailor hopped quickly out of the tree and pretended to be a little out of breath. "I could have gone on for miles!" he bragged.

At last the tailor arrived at the king's palace. When the king asked the tailor to prove his strength, Michael demanded some kind of payment. "I will give you my daughter in marriage and half my kingdom if you can kill the two mean giants who live in the woods." "Oh, that is an easy enough task!" said the brave little tailor.

When Michael saw the giants in the woods, they were sleeping under a tree. He picked up some rocks and climbed into the tree. Then he dropped a rock on one of the giants. The giant awoke and accused the other of hitting him. "Oh, you were dreaming. Go back to sleep," said the innocent giant. When they were both sleeping again, the tailor dropped another rock on the same giant as before. "This time I was not dreaming! You hit me again!" The innocent giant again denied doing anything. After the tailor dropped the third rock, the giant jumped up and grabbed the innocent giant and started wrestling around yelling that no one ever hit him and got away with it. They picked up huge rocks and clubs and fought until they knocked each other dead! Then Michael went back to the king and told him he had killed them easily. The king sent his servants to the woods to prove out the story, and they found the two dead giants.

The king was still not willing to give up his daughter and half his kingdom so easily. "Before I give you anything, you must prove yourself once again. Go back into the woods and capture the unicorn that is terrifying my people," demanded the king. "Oh, easily," said Michael.

The brave little tailor went back to the woods and walked a long time before he came upon the unicorn. Seeing the tailor, the unicorn ran with his horn pointing straight at him! Michael stood against a tree and remained there motionless until the unicorn was nearly upon him and then he jumped out of the way. The unicorn was running so fast that he could not stop and he ran his horn right into the tree and he was stuck! The tailor cut off the piece of the tree where the unicorn was stuck and led him back to the king.

But the king was not ready yet to give up his treasures. "Please, just one more thing. Go to the woods one more time and capture the wild boar that is eating the plants from our gardens," demanded the king. "Such a small task," bragged the brave little tailor, and set off. He walked a long time before finding the boar. He had such a good plan. He ran to an empty house standing nearby, ran through the small front door and then jumped out the side window. As he thought, the boar followed him at a dead run, tried to run through the door behind the tailor, but the door was not wide enough and the boar got stuck in it. Michael threw a rope around the boar's neck and proudly led him back to the king.

Now the king could no longer put him off. The king granted Michael half his kingdom and the brave little tailor and the king's daughter were married and lived happily ever after.

The End

THE BREMENTOWN MUSICIANS (47)

A farmer who lived in the country made his donkey carry corn to the mill every day, but the donkey was growing old and the farmer planned to be rid of him soon. The donkey, guessing what the farmer planned, ran away for he intended to spend the rest of his life in Brementown, as a musician.

The donkey had not walked far when he came upon an old brown hound dog. "Why are you lying in the middle of the road?" asked the donkey. "I have long chased the foxes, but I am getting too old to run as fast as I used to. My master was going to kill me and I ran off. Now I don't know where to go," moaned the dog. "Well, I have nearly the same story, but I am not going to lie around moaning. I am going to Brementown to become a musician. Why don't you come with me?" asked the donkey, and the dog agreed to go with him.

They walked down the road a bit and came upon a cat who was crying. They asked why it cried. The cat said, "I have chased mice from the barn for years, but now my teeth are not as sharp and I would rather eat something soft. So my mistress cast me out." So the donkey and the dog asked the cat to quit crying and come with them, and the cat followed them down the road.

The three of them walked on and came upon a rooster crowing so loudly that it hurt their ears. "My gracious, Rooster! Why do you crow so loudly?" the donkey asked. "My mistress is having company tomorrow for dinner and they intend to serve me to the guests. Since this is my last night to live, I intend to crow while I have a chance," explained the old rooster. "Nonsense! You are too good a singer to die. Why not come with us to Brementown and become a great singer?" asked the donkey. "Why, yes, I believe I will!" said the rooster and he followed the donkey, the dog and the cat.

As Brementown was too far away to make in one day, they stopped for the night in the woods. The donkey, the cat and the dog lay down under a tree, but the rooster flew up to the top. He looked around him from his high perch. "Hey, there's a small house with lights near here," he yelled. They all thought that whoever lived there might put them up for the night and the four of them marched off to find the house.

When they got near and heard loud voices, they peeked in the windows. "It looks like a band of robbers at the dinner table," said the donkey. The four of them came up with a good plan.

The donkey put his feet up on the window sill, the dog climbed up on the donkey's back, the cat climbed up on the dog's back, and the rooster flew up to sit on the cat's back. They all started singing, loudly. They donkey brayed, the dog howled, the cat meowed and the rooster crowed! Then they crashed through the window! The robbers, thinking that ghosts were after them, ran from the house as fast as they could go!

The animal friends laughed and went on in. They ate the remains of their dinner from the table. When they were tired, they put out the light. The donkey lay by the table, the dog lay behind the door, the cat lay by the hearth and the rooster flew up in the rafters.

After a time the robbers thought maybe the ghosts had left and sent one man to see if all was well. He sneaked quietly into the house and over by the hearth. Thinking the cat's eyes were two burning coals, he held a match close to them. But the cat jumped and hissed in the man's face. He tried to run, but the donkey gave him a swift kick and the dog bit him in the leg. The rooster screamed "Cock-a-doodle-do!"

The man ran back to the other robbers as fast as he could go. "There is some kind of monster in the house. When I went in, it breathed loudly in my face, then hit me with a club and then stabbed me in the leg. There was a judge high up and he yelled, "Bring him to me!"

So the robbers never went back to the house and the four friends liked the house so much that they stayed there and never did get to Brementown.

The End

THE BRONZE RING (19)

Once there lived a king in his palace with a very large garden. No gardener had been able to make anything grow on this land. The king sent his servants to find any gardener whose father and grandfather had also been gardeners. After a long search, such a man was found and brought to the palace. This young gardener produced beautiful fruit, vegetables and flowers. He took the best vegetables to the cook, the choicest fruits to the king, and the prettiest and sweetest flowers to the king's young daughter.

The king's daughter and the gardener were in love so when her father told her she was to marry the doctor's son, she wept. "I do not want to marry the doctor's son. I want to marry the gardener," she cried. The king was horrified to think his daughter should marry a common gardener! He told his daughter she must marry the better man of the two. He would send them both on a journey to a faraway place. The first man back would marry her.

Both men were called before the king and sent off on the journey. The doctor's son galloped off on a fine horse in fine clothes with his pockets full of money, but the poor gardener was sent off in rags on an old and lame horse.

In a few days the doctor's son came upon an old lady who begged for a ride to

the nearest town, but he did not want an old woman to slow him down and brushed her away and galloped on. Later the gardener came upon the old lady and asked her to ride along with him for he knew she was very weary.

When they arrived at the next town, servants of that land's king were running through the streets yelling, "The king is old and sick. Anyone who can cure him will receive great rewards!" The doctor's son paid no attention to the sick king, but galloped away on his fine horse. The gardener wished he could help the poor sick king, but how? Then the old lady whispered to him, "I will help you cure the king since you helped me along the way. Just do as I tell you."

The old lady had him kill three rats and burn them to ashes. He took the ashes to the king and said he could cure him if he would only trust in him. The king was frightened when he heard he would have to be put in a boiling pot of water, but somehow he trusted the man. The gardener got the water boiling in the big pot and spread the ashes of the rats next to it. Then he put the king in the boiling water ever so gently and cooked him till nothing was left but bones. He then spread the bones over the ashes and at once the king was revived, young and healthy again!

The king was overjoyed! "You may have half my kingdom and half my wealth!" cried the king. But the gardener remembered to do as the old lady had said. "No, thank you. I ask only for your bronze ring." The king did not want to part with the bronze ring for it was magic and would do anything asked of it. But had it not been for this young man he would not even be alive so he gave him the bronze ring. Immediately the young man told the ring, "Give me a fine ship filled with strong sails and a fine crew and then fill my ship with fine jewels and spices and at once the ship was there, exactly as he had demanded.

The gardener came upon the doctor's son who by now had been stripped to poverty in his journey as sometimes happens when thoughtless people think only of themselves. The doctor's son did not recognize the young gardener and thought him to be rich because of his fine clothes. He begged the gardener to help him. The gardener did recognize the doctor's son and said he would help the poor man if he would agree to be branded with his new bronze ring. "Yes" said the very sad man, "that would be agreeable if you will just help me get home." So the gardener heated the bronze ring and branded the distraught man, but then he gave him a small and ugly ship so he could sail home. And off sailed the branded doctor's son in his small, ugly ship.

The young gardener rested a few days and spent time visiting with relatives. A few days later he sailed his beautiful ship home and arrived at the town in his luxurious ship. He went straight to the king to ask for the hand of his daughter in marriage. But the king said, "No, I have promised the doctor's son to have my daughter's hand in marriage. He was the first to arrive back from the required journey!" The gardener asked, "Would you have a man marry your daughter that has worked for me and has my brand on his back?"

"No, I would not have such a man marry my daughter," said the king, but you must prove to me that he has your brand on his back." So the gardener lifted the shirt of the doctor's son and there, for the king to see, was the brand of the bronze ring on his back! So the king then decided to give his daughter in marriage to the rich gardener! The princes and the gardener were so in love and they lived happily ever after.

The End

THE DICKEY BIRD (63)

Once there was a very poor woman who lived in a very big cup and saucer. She loved to walk in the woods, and one day she found a bird with a broken wing. She took the hurt bird home with her and put a little splint on his little wing. In time the bird's wing was well and she took him back to the woods. Although the bird had never spoken a word in her home, he now said, "Thank you kind lady for taking care of me. Anything

you want, just ask me, and I can grant your wish. Just call out "Dickey Bird!" and I will come. But you must not come too often."

The lady went back home and sat and thought and thought. At last she jumped up and ran back to the woods. "Dickey Bird! Dickey Bird! Where are you?" she called. "Here I am," he answered. "What do you want?" "Oh, I should so much like to have a little house instead of that cup and saucer I live in." "You shall have it. Go home and see," he answered.

When she reached home, there was the cutest little house you ever did see. But, there was no furniture! She ran back to the woods and called to the bird. "Dickey Bird! Dickey Bird! Where are you?" "Here I am," he said. "What do you want?" "My house is very nice, but I really would like to have some furniture for it," she said. He agreed and when she got home, the house was furnished beautifully.

A few days later she went to the Dickey Bird again and asked for a garden. He agreed and when she arrived home, she had a beautiful garden full of vegetables, but there were already weeds. She ran back and asked for a gardener, and when she arrived home, the gardener was at work removing all the weeds.

In time, the lady tired of sitting alone in her new house with all its nice new furniture. She went back to the woods and called to the bird. "Dickey Bird! Dickey Bird. I am so lonely and want more than anything a little boy of my own." He told her to go home and she would find her new son.

The lady loved her new son. They had many good times together, but soon the boy asked for some toys. She went to the bird again and asked for some toys. "Yes, he can have some toys, but remember, do not ask for too much or you may lose all you have."

Soon the boy tired of the new toys and asked for a pony. The lady did not think this too much to ask and went to the bird and asked for the pony. "Yes, I can give him a pony, but remember what I said about coming too often." When she arrived home, the boy was already riding around on his new pony. Oh what a great time he was having!

The lady had treated the little boy so well, she soon had him very spoiled. He only had to ask for something, and he received it. Now he wanted something that no other little boy had. He went to his mother and asked her. At first she hesitated, but then she went to the bird and called out, "Dickey Bird! Dickey Bird!" He didn't appear so she had to call him again. At last he appeared. "What in the world do you want now?" he asked. "I only want one thing more, and it is not of this world. My son wants the moon to play with as his own." "Go home, go home!" screeched the bird.

When she reached her home, the little house was no longer there. Neither was her garden, her gardener, the pony, any toys, or even her little boy. All that was left was the cup and saucer that she had started with.

The lady never saw the Dickey Bird again. From that time on she learned she must be satisfied with what life gave her. Asking for too much can mean you can end up with nothing.

The End

THE DOG IN THE MANGER, A FABLE (12)

One evening a little dog was looking for a place to nap. He saw a manger full of fresh hay. "Oh, that will surely be a sweet, soft place to take a nap," he thought to himself, so he lay down and went to sleep.

Presently the cow came in for his supper. As he put his nose down into the hay, the little dog woke up. No one was going to eat his bed! He ran back and forth barking and snarling. The poor cow could not figure this out. He knew the dog ate biscuits and bones, not hay. Why would he want his hay? He was hungry and this was his supper.

Most animals would have fought for their supper, but this poor cow was getting old and did not have the strength to fight, so the cow began to cry. As his big hot tears rolled down his nose into the hay, the dog laughed. He did not laugh long though, for the wet tears soon had the hay all wet and the dog jumped out. Who wants to sleep in wet hay?

The End

Moral: You should not begrudge something to others that you cannot use.

THE ELVES AND THE SHOEMAKER (36)

There once lived a very poor shoemaker. He only had enough money to buy enough leather to make one pair of shoes at a time. When he sold one pair of shoes, it left him just enough money to buy a bit of food and just enough leather to make one more pair of shoes. He would cut out the shoes one day and sew them together the next day.

But one morning when the shoemaker went down to his workshop there stood a fine pair of shoes - already sewn together! He did not see how this could be. He remembered leaving them on the counter, only cut, not sewn together. He asked his wife if perhaps he had gotten up in the night and had been so sleepy that he had not remembered. She said she had not seen him get up in the night.

As soon as he sold the shoes he ran out to buy more leather. Since he had not spent an extra day sewing he had money enough to buy leather for two pairs of shoes. He spent the whole day working as fast as he could and he was able to cut out both pairs of shoes. He put the cut leather on the counter and he went to bed.

The next morning, again the shoes were already sewn together. The shoemaker ran to his wife. "Did you see me get up in the night?" he asked. She replied, "No, you were so tired that you had to have slept the whole night without waking."

The shoemaker soon sold the two pair of shoes and had enough money to buy leather for four pair of shoes and a bit of food. Again he only cut them out and went to bed. Again the next day the shoes were sewn together! Now he and his wife were confused!

This went on for days. Each day he cut out the leather and each night while he slept, the shoes were sewn together! He now was making good profits since he was not spending any of his time in sewing the shoes together. But the man could not stand not knowing who sewed the shoes each night. He said to his wife, "Tonight I am going to get up and see who is working in my workshop." His wife said she would get up and watch with him.

That night they put out the lights and watched from behind the door. In a little bit six tiny elves crept through the window and started working. Some were sewing, some were tapping on the heels with nails and a hammer and some were shining and polishing the finished shoes. They worked busily and sang happily as they worked! Such tiny elves they were! "Look, husband," whispered the wife. "They only have on such tiny bits of clothing. They must be cold."

The shoemaker and his wife went back up to their bed and spent the night talking and planning. The next day the shoemaker rose and put a sign in the window that said his shop was closed for the day. Then he went to work on six tiny shoes that would only fit the tiny elves. His wife busied herself making six tiny shirts, six tiny trousers and six tiny socks.

That night they put out the lights and watched from behind the door again. In a little while they saw the six tiny elves come in through the window. One of the elves spied the tiny shoes and clothes. "Look!" he yelled to the others. They all came running to see what he was shouting about. Delighted, each of them picked up a set of clothes and shoes and put them on. They all danced around admiring each other and exclaiming, "Look at me!" They did not work that night, only played and danced and sang happily.

With the help of the little elves, the shoemaker by now had saved enough money that his shop was quite profitable. He no longer had to worry about having enough money to buy leather or food. He was very grateful to the elves. From then on he never left any unsewn leather lying out at night and he never saw the elves again. But he knew that the tiny elves must be out there somewhere helping another poor shoemaker.

The End

THE EMPEROR'S NEW CLOTHES (32)

There was once an emperor who cared way too much about his clothes. He had a different suit of clothes for nearly every hour of the day. He spent most of his time changing into his new suits. The townspeople thought the king entirely too vain and he spent too much money on clothes, but they could do nothing about it.

One day two swindlers came to town. They told everybody they were weavers and could make the best cloth that anyone had ever seen. Better yet, they even had cloth that only the wisest people could see. If you were dumb or even a little slow, you would not be able to see the cloth. Of course, it was very expensive.

The king immediately sent for these swindlers he thought were real weavers. He wanted only the very finest clothes, but most of all, wanted a suit of clothes made from cloth that only the wise could see. "Get to work on them!" he screamed at the weavers. They winked at each other. "We must have some money in advance," they told the king. "At once no matter what the cost!" the king shouted, and paid them in advance.

The men went to the weaving room and pretended to take thread from their bags. Then they pretended to put the thread on their weaving looms. They pretended to weave, of course with nothing really on their looms, but seemed to be really hard at work. People about the palace watched through the windows and could see nothing on the

looms. Of course, if they said they could not see the cloth being woven, their neighbors would think they were stupid. So, instead, anyone that peered through the window would pretend to see the cloth and say, "Oh, isn't that beautiful cloth!"

The king thought this a good way to test his servants. If they came back and said they could not see the cloth, he would know they were too stupid to work for him. So he sent one after the other to the weavers to see the cloth and report to him how it looked. Each pretended to see the cloth, thinking they were the only person that could not see it, and assured the emperor the cloth was astounding!

At last the king decided to go himself to see the new cloth. Everyone he sent had come back saying how beautiful it was, so he would surely have no trouble in seeing it. When he arrived the weavers jumped up and bowed low before the king. "How do you

89

like the cloth, your majesty?" they asked. The king stared and stared but, of course, he could see no cloth. He was surely not going to let anyone think he was the only stupid person in the land, so he pretended to see it. "Why, that is the most beautiful cloth I have ever seen. Hurry and make it into a suit, and I'll wear it in the big parade this week!"

At last the day came and it was time for the parade. The two weavers brought in the pretend suit. They pretended to hold out the shirt and told the king to strip down to his underwear and get into the shirt. So the king pretended to put on the shirt. Next he pretended to put on the pants. Finally they brought in his royal train and his crown and the king went to line up for the parade. He felt very foolish standing there in only his underclothes and his train, but everyone kept talking about his beautiful new suit. If everyone else could see it, he had better keep quiet and pretend to be proud of the suit.

The parade started and the king marched along trying to look very proud. All the people kept yelling things about the king's beautiful new suit. "Oh, isn't that the most beautiful suit you have ever seen?" they asked each other. And, of course, everyone answered, "Oh, yes!" Everyone thought they must be the only stupid person in the land since everyone could see the cloth but them!

Suddenly a very small child stepped up and pointed to the king. "But, Mama, he has nothing on but his underwear!" Hush, you innocent, stupid child!" commanded the mother. Then another child agreed that indeed, the king did not have any clothes on. Finally all the people started laughing. Indeed, they were not stupid. The king really did not have any clothes on!

The king, of course, was very embarrassed, and the parade ended abruptly. The king had the two men imprisoned. He kept two of his suits and passed out all the rest of his clothes to the people of his country. From then on, the king realized that clothes were not all that important after all.

The End

THE FAIRY OF THE DAWN (15)

There was once a king named Isis who had three sons, Florea, the eldest, Costan, and Petru, the youngest. Now this king had two eyes, just like other kings, but his right eye was always laughing, while his left eye always wept. His sons wondered why his eyes were like this, but dreaded asking him, for whenever anyone approached the king with the question, he would go into a rage. Petru was determined to find out why his father's eyes were so odd and decided to ask, no matter what the outcome. So, Petru went to his father and asked. The king flew into his usual rage, but his left eye wept less after that! So he bravely asked his father again. The king again flew into a rage, but his eye wept even less after that! After asking a third time the king said that if his son was going to keep asking, he should tell him.

The king said, "My right eye laughs when I see my three strong sons, but my left eye weeps for fear of what will happen to my kingdom when I die. The only way to stop the curse is to bathe my eyes from the fountain of the Fairy of the Dawn. If one of my sons can get this water, I shall know he can rule my kingdom."

When Petru told his brothers, they knew they must try to get the water and decided among themselves that Florea, the eldest, should try. So Florea took his horse and left. He rode all day and all night. At last he stopped to rest and a huge dragon rose up before him and Florea rode home in fear for his life!

Costan was next to try. He rode two days and when he stopped to rest, just as with his brother, the dragon appeared. Costan was terrified and also rode straight back home.

Petru was last to go. When the dragon appeared before him, Petru did not run. He tried to fight but his horse kept rearing so that Petru could do nothing. He returned home to get a better horse. The stableman approached him. "Petru, I can help you. Go and get the bridle of your father's old horse, then strike it against the barn." Scarcely had Petru hit the barn with the bridle than a beautiful horse appeared! He was not just beautiful, but was a spirited magic horse that could talk! "I have been to the Fairy of the Dawn and I can help you," said the horse.

Petru and his magic horse soon came upon the dragon. "Listen to me," said the horse. "Draw your sword, I will leap over the dragon and you cut his head off when we are directly over him." Petru agreed to do as the horse said and they were quickly on their way.

After riding a few days they came upon a forest that was made of copper rather than wood. The trees, leaves and flowers were all pure copper. As they rode, the flowers cried out, "Pick me and you will have good luck." As Petru stopped to pick one the horse said, "Petru, do not pick any flowers. They are under a curse. If you pick one you will have to fight the Welwa, the horrible goblin." But Petru could not resist the pretty copper flowers and picked some. Suddenly the Welwa appeared! It was a horrible looking thing with a brown face like a bear, fangs like a vampire and two pointed ears. "Petru," said the horse, "the only way you can win is to take the bridle from my neck and throw it over his head." Petru fought with all his might for two days before he finally managed to fling the bridle on the goblin. As he did, it turned into a beautiful horse! "Oh, thank you, for you have broken the curse that was on me," said the beautiful horse.

Soon they came to another forest, but this forest was made of silver. As in the copper forest, the flowers begged to be picked. Even though the horse warned him against it again, Petru picked some silver flowers. Suddenly another Welwa appeared. It was even more horrible looking than the first. The battle raged on for three days before Petru managed to throw the bridle over this goblin. It too, turned into a horse and thanked him for ridding the curse.

One day Petru's horse stopped and said, "Petru, if we journey further this way, we shall enter the kingdom of the goddess, Mittwock. The air will get so cold, you cannot imagine. We cannot go unless we go completely to the house of Mittwock without ever stopping." The lad thought this seemed easy after what he had been through and they plunged on. It did indeed get cold, so cold that icicles hung from their hair. Along the road men stood warming themselves at fires, but they went on for days without stopping. Finally they came to the house of Mittwock.

The goddess at Mittwock welcomed them into her home and let them warm themselves. She gave Petru a small box and told him that any question he asked of it would be answered. He asked the box how his father was. "Your father is very angry with your brothers, for they wish to rule their father and his kingdom," the box said.

After many days of riding they came to the house of the goddess, Thunder. She welcomed them. "How much further to the Fairy of the Dawn?" asked Peru. The goddess told him he would have to stop and see the goddess, Venus, before he would reach the Fairy of the Dawn. When he was ready to leave, she said, "Stop back on your way home and I will give you something you will need." He promised to stop.

He rode on another day and reached Venus. They talked about the Fairy of the Dawn. "I was once the most beautiful girl in the land but as the years passed, the Fairy of the Dawn made my beauty leave and gave me wrinkles," she said. "If you can get me a cup of water from her fountain, I can get my beauty back. Take this flute with you because there are giants and monsters that would try to kill you. As long as you play this flute, it will lull them all to sleep." He thanked her for the flute and set about the final part of his journey. Nothing would stop him now!

As they neared the castle, Petru started playing the flute. All around him he passed sleeping monsters and giants. Inside he found the Fairy of the Dawn sleeping beside a fountain. Knowing this was the water he had come after, Petru filled his flask and left.

He stopped to give Venus some water and then stopped to see the goddess, Thunder. She gave him a strip of cloth and told him it would protect him from his brothers who were riding toward him to kill him and take the water to the king. Petru rode on as fast as the wind.

After days of riding he met up with his brothers and they did try to kill him, but the cloth protected him. They rode away in misery and were never heard from again. Petru took the water home to his father and cured his father's eyes. In time, the king died and Petru became the new king. Such a wise, good and brave king he was, too.

The End

THE FISHERMAN AND HIS WIFE (79)

A long time ago a poor fisherman and his wife lived in a small cottage. The man made a living by fishing in the sea each day and selling his catch in the city. One day he caught a great flounder. As he pulled the hook from its mouth, the flounder cried, "Oh, Fisherman, please throw me back. I am really an enchanted prince and would not taste good at all!" The fisherman wasn't about to eat an enchanted prince and threw it back into the sea.

When he arrived home his wife asked, "Did you not catch any fish today, dear husband?" He told her the story of the enchanted fish. "But, dear husband, you should

have asked for a wish. If the fish was enchanted, he could have granted you a wish. Go back and ask the fish for a better cottage."

The man did not want to go and ask a favor of a fish, but the woman begged her husband until at last he went back to the sea and called out to the flounder. "Flounder, Flounder. Jump out of the sea. My wife wants me to ask a favor of thee." The flounder jumped out and asked what the man's wife wanted. She wants to know if you can give us a better cottage," said the man. The fish replied, "Go back to your wife. She is in the new cottage now."

When he reached home, it was a new cottage! He and his wife were very pleased and lived happily in it for a time, but one day his wife begged him to go back and ask for a bigger house -- like a castle! The fisherman argued, but again his wife insisted. Knowing there would be no peace in his house, he went back to the sea. "Flounder, Flounder. Jump out of the sea. My wife wants me to ask a favor of thee." The flounder at once appeared and asked what his wife wanted. "Now she wants a castle!" said the man. "Go back, for she is in it now," said the flounder.

They were pleased with the new castle for a while, but one day the wife said to her husband. "With this castle, you should be king. Go and ask the fish to make you king." The man was astounded! He did not want to be a king! His wife screamed at him, "You are so foolish, you could not be king if you wanted to. Go and ask the fish to make me the king!" The man argued with his wife, but again in vain. He knew he would have to go or never hear the end of it. When he reached the sea he called out to the flounder. "Flounder, Flounder. Jump out of the sea. My wife wants me to ask a favor of thee." At once the flounder appeared. "What now?" the flounder asked. "My wife wants to be king!" said the man, still amazed at himself for even asking. "Go back. She is now king," said the flounder.

When the man reached home his wife was sitting on a throne with a crown on her head. The castle was even bigger than before and guards were all around her. He could not see how his wife could be a king, but she surely was! Servants, ladies in waiting, attendants of every kind were awaiting her words. Her throne was studded with diamonds and jewels. Princes and Dukes walked about importantly.

It wasn't long before she called her husband to her and said, "Go back and tell the flounder I want to be Emperor!" The poor man argued, but the wife said, "I am king and you will do as I say!" The man now had no choice.

The poor and embarrassed husband started off toward the sea. Overhead the sky turned very dark. When he reached the sea, lightning was tearing through the sky and the clouds rolled and thundered. The frightened husband called out to the flounder. "Flounder, Flounder. Jump out of the sea. My wife wants me to ask a favor of thee." When the flounder came to him, it snorted, "What does she want this time?" The man lowered his head and then said, "She wants to be Emperor." The fish looked at the man oddly and then said, "Go back to your wife. Now she has asked for too much. She has now returned to her old small cottage and you will find her there now!"

The End

THE FOX AND THE CROW, A FABLE (75)

The old black crow had found a piece of cheese and flew up into a tree to eat it. Along came a sly old fox. He sure would like to have that piece of cheese and he was just sly enough to get it for himself. He knew that this old black crow was very vain, thinking himself the best singer in all the land.

Good day, Mr. Crow," said the sly fox. The crow didn't say anything for he was munching on the piece of cheese. He wasn't going to share it with anyone for he deserved only the best for himself, he always thought.

"Mr. Crow, I have heard that you have the prettiest singing voice around. Please let me hear such a fine voice sing a beautiful song," said the sly fox.

Well, with such compliments coming from the old fox, the bird simply had to show off his voice. As he opened his mouth to sing, the cheese fell - straight into the fox's mouth!

The sly fox ran off, yelling back over his shoulder, "Hey, you stupid, vain crow. You should not brag about having one thing if it means losing another!"

The End

Moral: When someone flatters you, it may just be their way of getting the best of you.

THE FOX AND THE GRAPES, A FABLE (73)

In case you have ever wondered why people sometimes laugh and say, "Oh, sour grapes," I will tell you a short story that will tell you why.

An old fox lived near a fine grape yard. One day as he was out hunting for his breakfast, he decided on some ripe grapes. Oh, they looked so good! "You ripe, purple, sweet grapes, I am going to eat you for my breakfast," he chuckled and licked his lips.

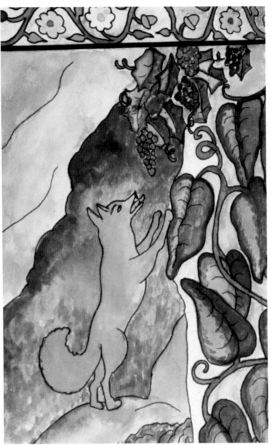

The grapes looked a little high, but not too high for him, he thought. He jumped up, but missed the grapes. Yes, they were a little high. Then he jumped again. Still he missed. He tried getting way back and taking a fast run at them but still he could not jump high enough. He spent the whole day jumping after those lush looking grapes, until he finally could jump no more.

The fox looked up at those beautiful, ripe grapes and snarled, "You stupid sour grapes, I wouldn't eat you if you fell right into my mouth!" And with those words, he stomped off. The fox really had no right to call the grapes a nasty name.

The End

Moral: Just because something is unobtainable or hard to get, it should be not called names or made to feel bad.

THE FOX AND THE LITTLE WHITE HEN (76)

The little white hen was so pretty and plump that a fox was always chasing her, hoping to catch and eat her. Each day as she went to the woods to get some chips to carry home in her apron for her fire, the fox chased her. One day the little white hen did not see the fox. "Maybe he gave up chasing me," she said to herself. "Thank goodness."

Actually, the fox had not given up. He had come up with a really good plan. Before he left home, he was so sure of catching her today he even put the water on to boil so it would be ready to cook her as soon as he got home. He hid behind her house and when she left he slipped inside.

When the little white hen returned, the fox jumped out, threw a gunny sack over her, slung the sack over his shoulder and headed for home. He ran along so fast that he got very hot and decided to stop for a quick swim. He put the sack down and tied the top tight.

"Help, help!" the hen called, but no one was around to hear her. Then she thought about her apron pocket. She always wore a little blue apron which had a big pocket. In the pocket she always carried her needle, thimble, thread, and a small pair of scissors. She took out the scissors and cut her way out of the sack! Then she put some rocks in the sack and sewed it back up.

When the fox came back he picked up the sack, threw it over his shoulders and headed for home. "My goodness, this sack seems awfully heavy. Oh well, she will make a good meal!" he panted.

When the fox got the heavy sack home, he was glad he already had the water boiling. He held the sack over the boiling water and untied the top. The heavy rocks splashed into the boiling water so hard that the hot water splashed all over the fox. He ran off howling into the woods. He never again tried to catch the little white hen.

The End

THE FROG PRINCE (69)

A long time ago there was a princess named Sheryl who liked to sit by a pond and throw her ball up in the air and catch it. But one day as Sheryl she sat throwing the ball up, she did not catch it. The ball dropped to the ground and rolled into the pond. The princess loved her golden ball and knowing she could never retrieve it from the deep pond, Sheryl began to weep.

Suddenly she heard a voice ask why she was weeping. When she opened her eyes, no one was near except a frog sitting on a water lily in the pond. "I am weeping for my ball rolled into the pond and I love it dearly. Could you get my ball for me?" she asked.

The frog looked sadly at the princess and then answered, "I will get your ball if you will promise to be my companion. You must let me come to the palace and eat at your table and sleep in your bed beside you." Sheryl thought that was the silliest thing she had ever heard. She couldn't imagine the thought of that ugly thing in her bed, but thinking he could never get out of the pond and up to the palace anyway, she promised him what he asked. So the frog jumped back into the pond and soon pitched her ball onto the ground. The princess grabbed up the ball and ran for the palace with the frog yelling behind her, "Come back and get me. You promised to be my companion!" Yet, Sheryl kept right on running.

The princess was eating her evening meal when there came a knocking at the door. Opening the door she found the ugly frog. "Remember you promised I could eat with you," said the frog, but Sheryl slammed the door and went back to the table.

The king had seen his daughter slam the door and let no one in. "Who was at our door?" asked the king. The princess then told her father the story. Sheryl wasn't about to let the frog in, let alone in her bed. But the king said, "When you make a promise, you must keep it. Let the frog in and bring him to the table." Sheryl tried to protest, but her father insisted. So she let the frog in.

"It's about time you kept your promise," said the frog. "Lift me up by your plate so I may eat with you." Again the princess protested, but her father insisted she do as the frog asked. When the frog finished eating he said, "Now take me up to your bed so I may sleep beside you." Sheryl could not bear the thought of the dirty frog sleeping on her clean bed and she begged the frog to go away. But her father and the frog insisted she must keep her promise. There was nothing for her to do but take the frog to her bed.

The next morning when the princess woke, there lay the most handsome man she had ever seen. "I am the frog," said the man. "I was once a prince, but long ago I was bewitched by an evil fairy. I had to remain a frog until one day a princess would let me be her companion at her table and in her bed. You have released me from the evil fairy's curse."

From that time on, Sheryl was very careful about what kind of promise she made, and once a promise was made, she kept it.

The End

THE FROGS AND THE COW, A FABLE (7)

A cow went to a pond one day to get a drink of water. The cow, being very big and clumsy, did not even notice when it stepped on a young frog and squashed it down into the mud.

It didn't take long for the young frog's father to see that he was missing. He asked his other children what had happened to the one young frog who was missing. "Oh, Father! A big monster stepped on him and killed him!"

The old father frog asked, "Was the monster as big as me?" They all agreed that it was bigger than him. So the old frog puffed himself up and asked, "Was it bigger than this?" They all agreed that he was bigger than that. So he puffed himself up some more. "Was it bigger than this?" They still agreed that it was bigger. So the old frog puffed himself up bigger and bigger and bigger until at last, he burst!!

And that was the end of the old frog.

The End

MORAL: Do not pretend to be something you are not.

THE GINGERBREAD MAN (20)

One day a woman was making gingerbread men cookies. When she took them out of the oven, one of the cookies jumped right out of the pan and ran out the door. "Stop, stop!' yelled the woman. But the cookie ran on down the road.

"Hey, Gingerbread Man, where are you going?" yelled a little boy. The cookie knew if he stopped the boy would eat him. He ran on down the road yelling, "Ha-ha. I run, I run as fast as I can. You can't catch me because I'm the Gingerbread Man!"

The cookie saw a cow and the cow called out, "Stop, stop! Come and graze with me." The cookie knew what the cow wanted and ran on, yelling, "Ha-ha. I run, I run as fast as I can. You can't catch me 'cause I'm the Gingerbread Man!"

Then the cookie came upon a horse. "Hey, you, stop! Come and talk with me," yelled the horse. But the cookie knew better. He ran on, singing, "Ha-ha. I run, I run as fast as I can. You can't catch me 'cause I'm the Gingerbread Man!"

Then the Gingerbread Man came upon a fox. The fox didn't yell at him. He just stared at him. "Ha-ha. I run, I run as fast as I can. You can't catch me 'cause I'm the Gingerbread Man!" The sly old fox asked, "Who wants to catch you?" Well that made the cookie stop. "Well, don't you want to eat me? Everyone else does!" said the Gingerbread Man. "No. I am going across the river to play with my friends. Want to come?" asked the fox. And the Gingerbread Man thought about it and answered "Well, I can't swim. The water would melt me." "Well, hop onto my tail and I'll carry you across," said the sly old fox.

That sounded like fun! The Gingerbread Man hopped onto the fox's tail and the fox swam out into the lake. "Hey, my tail is getting wet. Climb onto my back so you don't melt," said the fox. So the Gingerbread Man climbed onto the fox's back. In a few moments the fox said, "You better hop up onto my head for I can't keep my back up high enough any longer." As the Gingerbread Man hopped onto the fox's head, he slipped and slid right down the fox's nose - right into the fox's mouth! The sly old fox gobbled up the cookie without even getting his mouth wet!

The End

THE GOLDEN GOOSE (24)

Simpleton had two brothers. His eldest brother was Hans, and his younger brother was Karl. Simpleton was a good and kind young man, but his brothers were very selfish.

One day their mother packed Hans a lunch and sent him to the woods to chop wood. A little man came to Hans and asked for a bit of food, but Hans yelled at him to go away. He was not giving up any of his lunch. The man went away, and in a few minutes, Hans cut his own arm with the ax and had to go home.

When Hans arrived home his mother gave Karl the lunch and sent him to cut the wood. Karl, too, was approached for something to eat, but Karl also sent the beggar away. In a few minutes Karl cut his leg and had to be carried home.

Simpleton then begged to go and try. His brothers laughed. If they could not cut the wood, Simpleton surely could not! But Simpleton insisted he could do the job and his mother gave him the lunch and sent him on.

Simpleton, too, was approached by the same little man begging for food. Simpleton at once gave him the lunch. "I will gladly share it with you," he said. The little man thanked him and ate. As he was leaving he told Simpleton to chop down a certain small tree and he would find something wonderful at the roots.

Simpleton did just as the man said. There among the tree roots sat a golden goose! The man was gone, so Simpleton could not even thank him. He set off for town to stay the night at an inn.

At the inn, the innkeeper called for his three daughters to come and see the unusual golden goose. "How beautiful it is!" they cried. And, that night, while Simpleton was sleeping, the first daughter thought to get at the golden goose and pluck one of its feathers to keep. As the girl touched the goose her hand stuck to it! No matter how she tried, she could not let loose of it!

In a few minutes the second daughter came in. She had the same idea as her sister. When she saw her sister stuck to the goose she ran to pull her loose, but all she did was stick to her sister! Next the third daughter came in, and when she ran to help her sisters, she too became stuck. They wriggled and twisted, but none of them could get free!

The next morning Simpleton came to his goose and found all three girls stuck. There was no way to get them loose, so there was nothing to do but set out together. They left the inn with Simpleton carrying his goose and the three girls trailing behind!

They had gone only a short way when the mayor of the town saw them. "Girls!" he yelled. "You should be ashamed of yourselves running after a man like that!" And he ran to stop them, but as he grabbed hold of the last girl he stuck to her! "Let me loose!" he cried, but no one could free him. And, on they went.

In a little while the minister saw them. "How shameful for the mayor to be chasing after those girls!" he yelled, and ran to pull the mayor away. Of course, the minister stuck to the mayor!

That night they stopped at an inn and heard a strange story. The king had a daughter that could not laugh! He was so worried about her that he was offering her in marriage to any man that could make her laugh. As everyone had been laughing at them all day, Simpleton thought to give it a try.

The next day when they appeared before the princess, she laughed and laughed! She laughed so hard at the three girls, the mayor and the parson trailing along, all stuck behind the goose, that she nearly collapsed!

The king was happy to see his daughter laughing, but hated the thought of her marrying such a simple peasant. He called Simpleton to him and demanded, "You must prove your worth before you can marry my daughter. You must find a man who can drink a barn full of water.

Where could he find such a man? He went to the stump where he had found the goose. There sat a man weeping. He told Simpleton, "I am so thirsty. I drank a barrel of water, but that did not quench my thirst." "I can help you. Just come with me," said Simpleton.

They went to the king and were taken to a barn which was stocked full of barrels of water. The man drank all day until, at last, he finished every drop of the water. But, still the king did not want to marry his daughter off to this peasant. "You must bring me a man that can eat a mountain of bread before I will think you worthy."

Simpleton again went to the stump and found another man weeping. "I have eaten a barrel of rolls but am still hungry." "Come with me and I can help you!" said Simpleton.

They went to the king. The courtyard held a mountain of bread stacked 50 feet high. The hungry man sat down and ate every crumb of the bread. Still, the king held out. "One more thing you must do. You must bring me a ship that can sail over the land as well as water."

Simpleton did not hesitate. He ran straight to the stump. There sat the same little man that had told him to chop down the tree. "I was the same man that drank the water and ate the bread. Now I will help you again by giving you the ship you need, for you shared you lunch with me willingly."

When Simpleton took the ship to the king, he could not hold out any longer. If this peasant could bring whatever the king asked for, he surely was worthy of marrying his daughter. They were married soon after that and they lived happily ever after.

The End

THE GOOSE GIRL (70)

Once there was a queen who had promised her daughter, Caitlin, in marriage to a prince in a faraway land. "I'm sending a servant girl with you. She will ride a horse, but you will ride Falada, the magic horse who speaks," said the queen as she gave her daughter a farewell kiss. She placed a silver chain around Caitlin's neck. "This chain will keep you from harm," said the queen.

The princess and the servant girl rode toward the land of the prince. Presently they came to a stream. "Please get me a drink of water," asked Caitlin. But the servant girl told the princess to get her own water, for she wasn't going to serve her. So the princess got her own water.

After a time they came to another stream. Again Caitlin asked the servant girl to fetch her some water, and again the servant girl refused. Again the princess climbed down to get her own water. As she bent over the stream, the silver chains slipped from

her neck and floated away. Scared now of the servant girl and no longer having her silver chains to protect her, Caitlin spoke to the water, "What will become of me?" and the silver chain answered, *"Alas, alas, if your mother knew, her loving heart would break in two."* Then the servant girl mounted Falada and warned the princess. "Falada is the best horse and I choose to ride him. You ride my old nag or you will be sorry," she snapped. Caitlin was afraid to argue and climbed on the old nag horse.

They rode on for many days with the servant girl ruling the princess and being very mean to her. As they neared the palace the servant girl said, "Change clothes with me, for I am going to be the bride. Do this or I will see that you die," screamed the wicked girl. The princess, afraid of her, did as she was told.

Entering the palace gates dressed beautifully and on the grand horse, the servant girl was mistaken for the real princess. The prince went to her, but the king looked at Caitlin. "Who is the lovely girl with you?" the king asked. The false princess told him the girl was only with her to keep her company. "Give her something to do to keep her busy now," said the false princess. Then she turned to the prince and told him to have the horse, Falada, killed. "He is a mean and miserable horse," she lied. Actually she was afraid that Falada would speak and give her away.

When Caitlin heard Falada was to be killed she went to the groom who had the ugly job of killing the horse. "Hang Falada's head over the town gates and you shall have this gold coin," she begged. So the groom took the coin and hung Falada's head over the town gates.

Now Caitlin's job each day was to tend geese with Conrad, a servant boy. Each day as they went through the gates, Caitlin would look up and bid good morning to the horse's head. The horse always spoke back, *"Alas, alas, if your mother knew, her loving heart would break in two."* This made Conrad very uneasy. When they reached the fields, Conrad would try to steal a curl from her hair since she always took it down to comb it. Caitlin didn't like Conrad trying to cut her hair and spoke to the wind: *"Blow wind, blow. Toss his hat to and fro. Make him chase this way and that, till my hair is back under my cap."*

After three days Conrad went to the king and told him the girl teased him. He refused to tend the geese with her, but the king ordered the boy to go once more and the next day the king secretly followed them. The king watched them pass under the gates and heard Caitlin and Falada speak. He watched when Conrad tried to snatch a curl and saw the princess make the wind blow away his hat. Then he went back to the palace alone. He thought all day about this lovely girl who now tended his geese.

The king called Caitlin to him that evening and asked why she acted and spoke so strangely. "I cannot tell you or I will die," she cried. But the king begged her till she broke down and told him the whole story.

The night before the wedding, the king seemed in a friendly mood. He turned to the false princess and laughingly asked her, "What would you do if a servant turned on his master?" The false princess, not knowing she had been found out, answered, "I would lock him up in prison forever."

"You have just named your own punishment for deceiving your mistress!" roared the king. And the servant girl was thrown into prison. The prince and Caitlin were married and ruled the land happily together.

The End

THE LION AND THE MOUSE, A FABLE (29)

Mr. Lion was sleeping contentedly one afternoon. He felt something scratching around in his mane. As he reached up to knock it off, a tiny mouse fell down by his mouth. Huh, what a fine dinner you will make," said the lion.

The little mouse cried, "Please, Mr. Lion, do not eat me. I thought you were a haystack and only needed some hay to build my nest with. I would never have trespassed on your beautiful mane knowingly!"

Mr. Lion decided that the poor little mouse was so polite and scared that he would let him go. Besides, he wasn't big enough to make much of a meal. As he let the tiny mouse go, the mouse cried out to him, "Thank you, sir. One day I shall do you a favor for the mercy you have shown me."

"How could a little tiny mouse like you ever help a big lion?" laughed the lion and went back to his nap.

Not many days after that, some lion trappers were hunting in the woods. They didn't want to kill lions, but trap them and take them back to the city to sell to the zoo. It didn't take them long to find Mr. Lion's tracks. They tracked him down and threw a heavy rope net over him.

Mr. Lion took to really roaring. "How infuriating! Let me go!" he roared for all the world to hear. Now the little mouse that he had let loose only a few days before heard the roaring. He listened to which direction the roaring was coming from and ran toward Mr. Lion. He soon found Mr. Lion sitting there with the rope net all around him. When the men weren't looking, the little mouse ran over and gnawed at the ropes. He soon had every rope completely gnawed through! "Now, you can see how even a tiny mouse can help a big lion if he really wants to!" yelled the little mouse as he scampered off into the woods.

The End

Moral: No matter how small something is, it is able to help.

THE LITTLE IRON POT (45)

Once upon a time there was a very rich man with many servants who owned most of a small town. Nobody liked the rich man because he was unfair with everyone. He was the only person around who had plenty of clothes and plenty to eat. He charged taxes against all the townspeople which left them all very poor. In this little town were a poor farmer and his wife who had no idea where their next meal was coming from. The rich landowner would not give them any food or credit. All their food and money was gone now. All they had left was one cow. They decided they had to sell the cow to get

some food, so the man untied his cow and started into the city. "Don't make a stupid trade, but get plenty of money for the cow," his wife demanded.

The farmer trudged along and came upon a traveler. "Where are you taking that fine cow?" asked the traveler. "I am taking it to town to sell so we can buy some food," replied the poor farmer. "How much do you want for the cow?" asked the traveler. "I want ten dollars for this fine cow," replied the farmer. "Well, I don't have ten dollars, but I do have this magical iron pot!" the traveler said. The farmer did not think the little iron pot worth ten dollars. Just then the little iron pot spoke up, "Take me home with you and I will take care of you!" Oh my gosh! A talking pot! The farmer made the trade and rushed home to his wife.

When he arrived home, his wife was angry that he made such a stupid trade, but then the little pot started talking, "I skip, I skip, as fast as I can!" "Where do you skip to?" asked the farmer's wife. "I skip to the house of the very rich man!" the pot said, and off it skipped! "Come back, come back!" yelled the farmer and his wife, but the little iron pot kept on skipping down the road. In a short while the pot was back and was full of food from the rich man's house! The poor farmer and his wife ate quite a few fine meals from the food in the pot and even shared it with their poor neighbors.

A week later the pot sang out again, "I skip, I skip as fast as I can!" "Where do you skip?" asked the farmer. "I skip to the house of the very rich man," it sang out and off went the little iron pot down the road again. When the little iron pot came back it was full of wheat! They pulled some wheat out of the pot, but each time they did, it seemed to refill itself! Soon the entire house was filled with wheat! They had so much wheat! They started baking bread as fast as they could and baked enough bread to last them and their neighbors a very long time.

A week later the little iron pot started singing again, "I skip, I skip, as fast as I can!" "Where do you skip this time" asked the farmer's wife. "I skip to the house of the very rich man!" it sang, and off it ran down the road! In a little while it returned and this time it was full of gold coins! As they pulled out gold coins, more and more seemed to fill up in the little iron pot! Soon gold coins were all over their house and out in the front yard! They had so much money that they were able to share it with all their neighbors and it would last everyone in town for many years to come!

After the pot was empty, the little iron pot sang out to the farmer, "I skip, I skip as fast as I can, I skip back to the house of the very rich man!" and off it skipped. A short time later the little black pot came skipping down the road with the very rich man in the pot! This time he didn't stop but kept skipping on by. As he passed the farmer's house the little black pot yelled out, "I skip, I skip as fast as I can! I skip to the far north with the very rich man!"

The End

THE LITTLE MERMAID (6)

About a hundred years ago there lived a sea-family, way down in the bottom of the sea. These sea-folk were like humans, only they had tails like a fish instead of legs. The boys were called mermen and the girls were called mermaids. The Sea King's wife was dead but he lived with his mother and his six mermaid daughters. They were all pretty but the youngest, Layla, was the prettiest of them all and had the sweetest voice. When Layla sang, all the fishes gathered around her to listen!

The mermaids' grandmother told them about the people, ships, trees, animals and grass that all lived above the water. When Layla was sixteen years old she would be allowed to go to the surface of the water and see such things for herself. It was so hard to wait! As each of her sisters turned sixteen they would swim to the surface and spend the day sitting on a rock, watching people pass in ships, or they would swim close the land and watch children playing. It was hard being the youngest and waiting so long, but at last her sixteenth birthday came and she was off!

Layla swam to the surface. She noticed how hot the sun was and had to splash water on her face and arms to cool them. In the distance she could see the city and the

King's palace. She saw birds flying above and butterflies flying by. How wonderful! Then she saw a big ship coming toward her. She swam close and peeped in the windows. The people were singing Happy Birthday to the prince!

The clouds above were dark and the wind began to blow, softly at first, then harder. The rain started falling and the lightening streaked across the sky. The little mermaid was not frightened but the people in the ship were rushing about, for the ship was rocking to and fro. The thundered roared and now some of the people on the ship were yelling in fear! And then lightening hit the ship and it split in half! The people splashed about in the water screaming in terror!

Layla remembered that her grandmother said people cannot live in water as the fishes and mermaids do for they drown and die. She could not save them all, but the prince was in trouble and she swam to him. She held his head above the water and then swam toward land with him in her arms. She laid him on the shore and sat by his side. He never opened his eyes, yet she knew he was alive. When she heard footsteps coming Layla slid into the water and swam behind a rock to watch. A girl and her friends came upon the prince, frightened at first to see him lying there. Somehow they revived him and the young mermaid saw his beautiful blue eyes open before they carried him away.

At last Layla swam back into the sea to her family. She went straight to her wise grandmother and asked, "Since the prince did not drown, will he live forever?" Her grandmother explained, "No, he will not live forever, but his soul will. Fish do not have souls but live for around three hundred years and then we simply die. Humans are not that way. Their body dies and is buried, but their soul rises to live with the Creator of all men and fishes."

Well, the mermaid was confused. "I want to have a soul and live forever too. Can I do that?" she asked. Her grandmother shook her head. "The only way you can get a soul is to get a man to love you more than anything. If he loves you enough to ask you to marry him, you will receive a soul. But to do that you would have to go to the Sea Witch first and get her help. Don't worry about it, for you would be much happier here in the sea for three hundred years than to have to grow legs and make someone love you that much," said the grandmother sadly.

That evening Layla found the Sea Witch sitting among rocks, bones and snakes. Fishes did not swim near her. But this little mermaid was determined, and asked, "Can you help me get a soul?" "Yes, I can help you, but you must give me what I want - your sweet voice. If you do that, I will help you grow legs and gain your soul," cackled the Sea Witch.

The poor little mermaid was frightened, but she agreed. The Sea Witch brewed a magic potion. "Take this and swim up to the surface of the water and sit on the shore. Drink this potion and your tail will split in half and become legs. Now I must have your voice," and with that she took the mermaid's sweet voice.

Layla swam back to her own home. Since she gave her voice to the Sea Witch, she would not be able to speak now. She did not know how to say goodbye but blew a hundred kisses toward her family. The little mermaid swam cautiously to the surface of the water, sat on the shore, drank the potion and fell sleep.

The next morning the prince found the mermaid on the shore. He asked where she came from, but Layla, who now looked like any other girl, could not speak. Not only was her voice gone, but her tail was now two legs! Such awkward things! He helped Layla to her feet and took her to his castle.

Time went by and even though Layla could not speak, the prince knew she loved him and he grew to love her very much. But, there was no way he could ever marry her for his father had promised him in marriage to the girl who had found him on the shore the day he should have drowned. There was no way he would ever know that Layla had helped him to the shore and saved his life, not the other girl.

There was nothing the Layla could do now. The wedding day was near at hand. She knew that on his wedding day she would die. She was not afraid to die, but she had wanted to marry him and earn her soul. The evening before his wedding, Layla went to stand by the water and watch the moon go down the last time. With the first rays of the sun, she knew she would die. At last she saw the sun beginning to rise. Now the sun was up! She saw strange beings flying about. Heavenly voices were singing and clouds were all about her. "Where am I?" Layla asked. A voice answered, "You are with the Bodies of the Air. We do not have souls yet because we have not fully earned them. We must spend three hundred years here being tested before we can go to live with our Creator. We can make the time go faster whenever we watch children. If a child laughs, one day is taken off our time, but if a child cries, one day is added to our time."

And since this story began one hundred years ago, the little mermaid now has about two hundred years to go, unless she can work away part of the time by watching the smiles of children. Children all over the world can help her by not crying, but smiling!

The End

THE LITTLE OLD WOMAN AND HER PIG (78)

One day a little old woman was sweeping her floor and found a dollar. "Just the amount I need to buy a pig," she said to herself. She put on her blue coat and her red hat and grabbed up her purse and was off for town. There she bought a nice fat pig. She started for home and the pig followed along nicely until they came to a fence, or what some people call a stile. The pig refused to go over the stile. She couldn't lift him over and no matter how she begged, the pig would not move. Then she saw a dog. She said to the dog, "Dog, dog, bite the pig! Pig won't jump stile and I shan't get home tonight." But he would not bite the pig.

She found a stick. She said to the stick, "Stick, stick, beat dog! Don't won't bite pig and pig won't jump stile and I shan't get home tonight." But the stick would not help beat the dog.

She went on and found a fire. She said to the fire, "Fire, fire, burn stick! Stick won't beat dog, dog won't bite pig, pig won't jump stile and I shan't get home tonight." But the fire wouldn't help her either.

She went on and found some water. She said to the water, "Water, water, put out fire! Fire won't burn stick, stick won't beat dog, dog won't bite pig, pig won't jump stile, and I shan't get home tonight." But the water would not help.

She walked on and met an ox. She said to the ox, "Ox, ox, drink water! Water won't put out fire, fire won't burn stick, stick won't beat dog, dog won't bite pig, pig won't jump stile and I shan't get home tonight." But the ox was not thirsty and would not drink.

She walked further still and met a butcher. She said to the butcher, "Butcher, butcher, kill ox! Ox won't drink water, water won't put out fire, fire won't burn stick, stick won't beat dog, dog won't bite pig, pig won't jump stile and I shan't get home tonight." But the butcher did not want to kill the ox.

She went a bit further she met a rope. She said to the rope, "Rope, rope, hang butcher. Butcher won't kill ox, ox won't drink water, water won't put out fire, fire won't burn stick, stick won't beat dog, dog won't bite pig, pig won't jump stile and I shan't get home tonight." But the rope just curled up and would not help.

She walked on and met a rat. She said to the rat, "Rat, rat, gnaw rope! Rope won't hang butcher, butcher won't kill ox, ox won't drink water, water won't put out fire, fire won't burn stick, stick won't beat dog, dog won't bite pig, pig won't jump stile and I shan't get home tonight." But the rat ran off and would not help.

As she walked on she met a cat. She said to the cat, "Cat, cat, kill the rat! Rat won't gnaw rope, rope won't hang butcher, butcher won't kill ox, ox won't drink water, water won't put out fire, fire won't burn stick, stick won't beat dog, dog won't bite pig, pig won't

jump stile and I shan't get home tonight." And the cat said, "Well, at the moment I am very thirsty. Bring me a saucer of milk and then I will kill the rat."

So the little woman ran to a cow standing nearby. She asked for some milk, but the cow said, "I will give you some milk if you will bring me a handful of hay first," so she ran to a farmer and asked for the hay. "I will give you the hay if you bring me a bucket of water," he answered. The woman grabbed up the bucket and ran to fill it with water. She brought it back to the farmer and he gave her the hay. She ran with the hay to the cow, who in turn gave her the milk. She ran with the milk to the cat and the cat lapped it up. "Now I am ready to kill the rat," said the cat.

So the cat ran as though to kill the rat, the rat ran and began to gnaw the rope, the rope ran to try to hang the butcher, the butcher grabbed an axe and ran to kill the ox, the ox hurried off to drink some water, the water tried to put out the fire, the fire began to burn the stick, the hot stick began to beat the dog, the dog jumped up and bit the pig and the pig jumped over the stile!

The End

THE LITTLE POT THAT WOULD NOT STOP BOILING (48)

A little girl and her mother were poor and often did not have enough to eat. The mother asked the little girl to go to the woods and pick berries for their supper. The little girl met an old woman who asked why she was in the woods. "My mother and I don't have any food and I am picking berries for our supper." The kind lady's eyes twinkled as she handed her a little iron pot. "Here. Take this little magic pot home. When you want something to eat, just say "Cook little pot, cook" said the old woman. When you want it to stop cooking, just say, "Stop little pot, stop." The little girl thanked the kind woman and skipped home to her mother to tell her about this new magic iron pot. That evening the little girl said, "Cook little pot, cook" and it cooked soup. When it made enough she said, "Stop little pot, stop" and it did. They thought it was the best soup they had ever eaten.

The next day, while the little girl was out playing, her mother wanted to fix more soup for lunch. "Cook little pot, cook" said the mother, and it magically filled up with soup. Quickly it filled to the brim and started spilling over. "Halt little pot, halt!" said the mother, but it did not halt and kept spilling onto the floor. "Quit pot, quit!" said the mother, but still it kept spilling and was now covering the floor and started flowing out the front door! "Stop it, quit boiling!" she yelled, but it just kept running out the yard and down the street! "Stop cooking, stop cooking!" she screamed at it, but the pot just kept cooking and it was now running through the neighborhood! The mother just could not remember the right words to make it stop!

When the soup reached the little girl she knew what was happening...her mother had forgotten the words to make the pot stop cooking! Neighbors were scooping up the soup! She waded through the soup running down the street. When she reached the kitchen, her mother stood wringing her hands and shouting all kinds of words at the little iron pot. "Stop little pot, stop!" yelled the little girl, and it did.

The End

THE LITTLE RED HEN (28)

The Little Red Hen and her chicks were scratching around the barnyard for food one day. "Oh, look my little ones, a grain of wheat" I shall plant it and one day we shall have bread from it."

When the wheat was ripe and golden she went to her friends in the barnyard. "Duck, will you help me reap my wheat." Not I," said the duck. "I am going swimming."

The Little Red then went to her friend, the cat. "Cat, will you help me reap my wheat? But the cat just yawned and stretched. "Not now, I am tired and just want to curl up and take a nap," purred the cat.

She then went to the pig. "Pig, will you help me reap my wheat?" "Oh no, I must take a bath now for I have been wallowing in the mud."

"Well then I will do it myself," said the Little Red Hen. She worked and worked, but she reaped the wheat by herself. Now it was time to take it to the mill to be ground into flour. Maybe she could get some help with this.

"Will you help me get this wheat to the mill to be ground into flour, Duck?' she asked. "Not I, for I am going to fly high in the sky," quacked the duck.

"Will you help me get this wheat to the mill, Cat?" "No, I am going to sharpen my claws," meowed the cat.

"Pig, will you help me get this wheat to the mill?" "No, I must eat my lunch now," oinked the pig.

"Well then I will do it myself," said the Little Red Hen. Then she put the wheat into a wheelbarrow and she and her little chicks trudged the long road to the mill." The miller ground the wheat into flour. Now it was time to go home and bake some bread from the flour.

"Duck, will you help me bake my bread?" she asked. "Not now," quacked the duck. "I am going to the pond with my friends."

Will you help me bake my bread, Cat?" she asked. "Oh, no. I am ready for another nap," purred the cat.

"Pig, everyone is too busy to help me bake my bread. Will you help me?" she asked. "No, I am trying to uncurl my tail," oinked the pig.

"Well then I shall do it myself," said the Little Red Hen. And she did. She kneaded and punched the dough and put it into her little oven to bake. What a delicious smell it made. "Now, who has time to help me eat the bread?" she yelled out over the Barnyard.

"I will!" yelled the duck and he waddled as fast as his little legs would go! "I will!" yelled the cat and he came on a run. "I will!" yelled the pig and he ran so fast his tail uncurled!

"Oh no you won't," said the Little Red Hen. I planted the seed by myself. I reaped the wheat by myself. I took the wheat to the mill with only my chicks to help me. I baked the bread by myself. Now my chicks and I will eat the bread by ourselves." And they did.

The End

THE NECKLACE OF PRINCESS FIORIMONDE (81)

Princess Fiorimonde was a pretty girl, but wicked and vain. She was old enough to be married, but had not found any man she considered good enough. Her father, the king, said there would be a party every night from now on until the princess had a chance to meet every man in the land.

Now, Princess Fiorimonde did not want to marry any man. She went to a witch. "Please help me. I do not want to marry any man because none are good enough for me. I will pay you well," she told the witch. The witch accepted the money and put a gold necklace around Fiorimonde's neck. "Just get the man to touch this necklace and you will be done with him. Be careful never to touch it yourself."

That night at the party, a young man seemed interested in the princess. He followed her out into the garden. Princess Fiorimonde certainly did not want to marry this man and began telling him about how pretty her necklace was. She asked him to feel how fine it was. As he touched the necklace, he vanished, but on the necklace appeared a small white pearl!

The next night, another man followed Fiorimonde into the garden, and he, too, touched the necklace, vanished, and another pearl appeared on the necklace. This kept on each night for a week. People were beginning to wonder where all the young men were disappearing to.

Now Girsha was the servant of Fiorimonde. She always helped Fiorimonde to dress and fix her hair. Girsha noticed the gold necklace the first day Fiorimonde wore it and could not understand why each morning there was a new pearl on the necklace. She thought about all the men that disappeared. After more thought, Girsha knew the necklace must have something to do with it. She went to town and found her friend, Omar. She told Omar what she suspected and asked if he could try to prove the princess guilty. He must be very careful.

That night, Omar friend hid behind a tree in the garden and watched Fiorimonde as she went there with another man. He saw the man touch the necklace, disappear and a new pearl was formed on the necklace! After Fiorimonde went back inside, Omar went to her. He invited her outside to the garden and started telling her about what a pretty necklace he had around his own neck.

"My necklace is prettier and much softer than yours," Fiorimonde said. "Oh, no." Omar responded, "mine is made of the finest wood and is very expensive." "Touch my necklace and see how fine it feels," said the princess.   "No, I would not want to touch such an ugly necklace as that!" Omar laughed.

Now Princess Fiorimonde was angry! Not only would the man not touch her necklace, he even thought it ugly! She reached up and grabbed her necklace and tore it from her neck. At once, Fiorimonde vanished and a bright red pearl appeared on the end of the necklace.

Girsha and Omar went to the king and told him about Fiorimonde and her necklace. Of course, the king found this hard to believe, but the people insisted they see the necklace. They all went out into the garden where the necklace was laying on the ground. The king picked up a stick and one by one he slid the white pearls off. Each white pearl turned back into a young man again. When the king realized the story must be true, he left the red pearl on the gold necklace and there Fiorimonde stayed.

The End

THE NOSE (17)

Three soldiers, Johnethen, Kona and Cau'i had fought in the war and were on their way home together and stopped in the woods to spend the night. After a few minutes a strange little man came up to them. "I have a present for each of you," he said, and he handed out the presents. He gave Johnethen a cloak and told him that whoever wore it would get anything he wished. He gave Kona a purse that would always be full of gold. Cau'i received a horn that made anyone who listened to it, do whatever the player asked.

The next morning Johnethen put on his magic cloak and wished for a fine castle. It immediately appeared before them, complete with gardens, fountains, furnishings and food! They thought they had all they could wish for and spent much time in their castle playing and eating anything they wanted.

One day they tired of staying at home and went out to meet their neighbors. They stopped at a nearby castle where a king lived with his daughter, Hera. Now Hera was a very pretty thing, but very wicked. All three men fell in love with her right away and had soon told her all about their magic pieces. Before they left the castle, Hera had somehow stolen each magic piece! The three men soon missed their magic cloak, horn and purse. Johnethen admitted about telling Hera, so they knew she must have stolen them. They turned right around and went back to the castle. Of course, Hera denied stealing anything, and as they could prove nothing, they had to leave without their magic pieces.

The three men decided to split up and each go their own way. Johnethen sat down under an apple tree to rest while the other two started off together. He reached up to pick some apples and ate them. Suddenly he reached to scratch his nose and found his nose had grown! Within moments it had grown down to his chest and then to his toes! It kept on growing so fast that he soon could not even see the end of it! "My goodness," Johnethen cried, "will it never stop growing?"

Meanwhile Kona and Cau'i were still walking. The nose soon caught up with them. They stared at it. "That looks like the end of a nose!" Kona cried. "Let's follow it back to see where it comes from." They followed the nose all the way back to their friend, Johnethen! "What happened?" Kona and Cau'i cried. "Can we do anything?"

121

Just then the little strange man came again. "Oh, I see you ate some of those awful apples that make noses grow! I can help you make it small again, though. Pick a pear from that nearby tree and eat the whole pear and your nose will grow back the way it was!" he chuckled. As soon as he ate the pear, his nose, did indeed, grow shorter. It kept getting shorter until, at last it was back to its normal size.

The three men discussed this among themselves and decided to try the cursed apples on the girl. Johnethen dressed himself up as a gardener and went to the palace. He said he had apples that were grown especially for the king's daughter. She was delighted that someone had grown special apples just for her and at once she ate the first apple, and also, at once, her nose started growing. It grew so fast and so long that no one knew where it ended!

The king offered great rewards for anyone who could cure his daughter of the unsightly nose. Now, Johnethen went back, not as a gardener, but as a doctor. He said that he knew of her stealing the magic articles, and if she would give them back, he could cure her. At first the girl did not believe him, but after he gave her several different things to eat, among them a small piece of the pear, her nose did start getting a little shorter. But then it quit shrinking. She finally gave him the magic cloak, purse and horn and he gave her the rest of the pear and her nose got smaller again. Her nose did finally get back to its normal size, but somehow she never did look quite as pretty as she had once been.

The End

THE OLD BLACK ROOSTER (61)

The old black rooster had always been a troublemaker. No matter how often the farmer told him to behave, he still made trouble. One night the farmer and his wife were sitting down to supper when they heard a loud noise out in the barn. "I better go see what is going on!" the farmer said to his wife. When he arrived at the barn the horse was kicking the stall and neighing as loud as he could. The cow was mooing. The pig was oinking. Such a noise you have never heard!

The farmer asked the horse, "Horse, what's the matter with you?" "There's an Indian coming to shoot us!" the horse neighed. "Who told you that?" asked the farmer. "Why, the cow told me," he neighed and continued kicking the stall door.

The farmer went to the cow that was mooing louder than he had ever mooed before. "Cow, shut-up! Why are you mooing so loud?" asked the farmer. "The Indians are coming to kill us!" mooed the cow. "Who told you that nonsense?" asked the farmer. "It's not nonsense, the pig told me!" the cow mooed, and he ran off to find a better hiding spot.

The farmer went to the pig who was so scared his tail had uncurled and was standing straight up on end! "Pig, who told you the Indians are coming?" "The old black rooster told me!" the pig oinked.

"Rooster, come here!" And just who told you the Indians are coming to kill you?" roared the farmer. "Well, nobody, but I did hear a big noise!" said the rooster as he stood scratching one toe in the dirt. "Oh, you dumb rooster, that was the cannon going off in town to celebrate the Fourth of July. What's that got to do with any Indians?" yelled the farmer. "I want this stopped right now! I am getting tired of all the trouble you are always starting!"

The very next day, the noise started again. The farmer talked to each animal again and the source, as usual, came down to the old black rooster just causing more trouble. That night the animals were so quiet you hardly knew they were around. They walked around trying to find the old black rooster, who seemed to have disappeared. Nobody knew where the old black rooster was except the farmer and his wife who were sitting down to a nice chicken dinner!

The End

THE PIED PIPER OF HAMELIN (42)

Once, long ago in a small town called Hamelin, there lived many rich people. They enjoyed living in fine houses and eating the best foods. There was only one poor family and that was a widow and her son, Tommy. Not only were they poor, but Tommy was lame and could only walk with a crutch.

One day some rats ran down the street and hopped onto a table full of cheese. The people shooed them away, but then here came some more rats and they hopped up into an apple cart. The people ran to shoo them away, but more came running. No matter how many rats they chased away, more came. Soon the town was overrun with rats. They ran in and out of the shops and houses. They climbed in and out of the cellars and pantries. The rats were eating up everything in sight! So a group of people went to the mayor and demanded to know what he was going to do about the rats. "I will think of something soon," answered the mayor. Then he called his councilmen together and they talked and talked, but none of them could figure a way to rid the town of the rats.

During the middle of their talks, a stranger came in. He wore a high, pointed, green hat and carried a flute. "I have come to help," said the stranger. "My name is the Pied Piper. I have a magic flute that will charm the rats. All I ask is 100 pieces of silver for payment." The councilmen and the mayor all laughed at the Pied Piper. "No one can charm rats, but if you can, you will receive 100 pieces of silver."

The Pied Piper went into the street and played music on his magic flute. Rats came running from every direction. He walked down the street and the rats all followed. He walked out of town and out to the river. He walked way out into the water, all the way up to his waist and then stopped, but the rats followed him right into the water and they all drowned!

The people all cheered and followed the Pied Piper back to the mayor. "Well, I know we said we would pay you 100 pieces of silver, but you did that so easily, don't you think that 50 pieces of silver would be plenty of payment?" said the mayor. The Pied Piper frowned and answered, "No, you don't get off so easily. I asked for 100 pieces and that is what I expect. If I am not paid the 100 pieces of silver by tomorrow morning, everyone will be sorry." And he stomped out the door.

Tommy ran up to him. "Mother and I haven't much, but we would like for you to come and have supper with us." So the Pied Piper went to their house. When he told Tommy and his mother about the mayor not paying him the money he had asked for, Tommy's mother offered him what little money she had. "Oh, no, good lady. But, if he does not pay me tomorrow, you are not to worry about what I will do, for you have been kind to me."

The next day the mayor still refused to pay the 100 pieces of silver. So the Pied Piper picked up his flute and began to play. Everywhere the children stopped playing and came running to him. They came out of every shop and every house, every child in the town. The Pied Piper bewitched the children, just as he had the rats, and they followed him down the street and straight out of town. The people ran after them, but the children did not seem to hear anything but the music of the flute.

Tommy was also running along with the children, but as he was lame, he could not quite keep up with the others. The Pied Piper led the children up to a mountain where a door opened up in the side of it. The children followed the Pied Piper right through the door, and it closed. Tommy was lagging so far behind that when the door of the mountain closed, he was left standing outside, the only child that did not enter. The people had to go back to their town, a town that only had one child left in it, Tommy.

The End

THE PRINCESS ON THE GLASS HILL (64)

Once upon a time there was a farmer who always had a good crop of hay but in the past three years on Halloween, something had always come and eaten the crop in one night. This year he asked his three sons, "Who would like to watch the barn on Halloween night to see what happens to our hay?" The oldest son shouted, "I'm the eldest son and I will watch!" That night he only waited a short while when the earth began to tremble and shake! He lost no time in getting back to the house! Of course, the next day all the hay was gone!

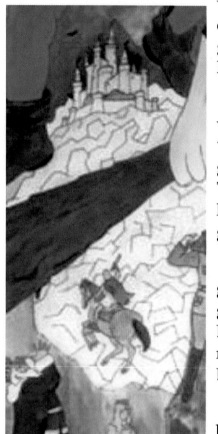

The next year the man asked his sons again who would go watch the hay. "I shall go," yelled the second son. "No one will get the hay this year!" That evening the ground began to tremble and shake just like an earthquake! That woke him up and you should see how fast that boy ran home! When they returned the next day, all the hay was gone again!

By the next year the two older boys did not want to go watch the hay, but the youngest boy, Dylan, wanted to go. The father said, "Oh, no, you are too young." But Dylan begged, "Father, please let me try." Well somebody needs to see what is happening to the hay, so the father let Dylan go.

Dylan had been watching about two hours when the barn began to shake! Dylan was frightened, but he did not leave. He could not stand to have his older brothers laugh at him. The ground shook for a time and then stopped. The boy relaxed and then he heard chomping, like something was eating and there stood a beautiful horse with a silver saddle and bridle. A silver suit of armor lay on the ground. Dylan took the horse to a secret place that only he knew about. He went home and told them everything was as it should be and the hay was saved this year.

The next year Dylan went back. The same thing happened. The barn and ground trembled and shook, then became still. Another horse was now eating, but this one had a gold saddle and bridle and a gold suit of armor was lying on the ground next to the horse. Dylan hid this horse in the same place where he had been keeping the first horse. He went home again and only told them the hay was saved. His brothers had almost quit laughing at him by now, but he was still younger so they still teased him.

About this time the king was going to have a contest. The palace was near a great hill that was made of glass. No person had been able to ride up the glass hill for it was very slippery and high. The king said that whoever could ride all the way to the top and retrieve the two golden apples from his daughter, who would be sitting on the very top, would be allowed to marry her. The contest would last two days or until someone could get to her and retrieve the apples.

When the contest started, all the men tried and tried to ride up the hill. It seemed impossible to climb. When they came to a slippery part, they slipped right back down. The king was about to call off the contest when a knight rode up on a horse. He wore a suit of silver and his horse had a silver saddle and bridle. He rode half way up the hill and waved at the princess. She was so impressed that she threw him one of the golden apples.

The second day many men tried again, but to no avail. No one could get their horse up that slippery glass hill. Just then a knight with a gold suit of armor with a red cape rode up on a beautiful horse with a gold saddle and bridle. He rode all the way to the top of the glass hill and snatched the second golden apple from the princess. Fast as the wind, he rode back down and straight out of sight.

The king was upset that anyone should not want his daughter and would ride off with the golden apples. He ordered all the people to come to the palace, line up and empty their pockets. Everyone did but nobody had the apples. The king asked if anyone was left who had not emptied their pockets. Dylan's older brothers laughed, "We have a young brother at home but he would not have them as he is too young and foolish." But the king ordered, "Go and get him just the same."

The brothers told Dylan to come and ran back to watch the fun. "Empty your pockets!" ordered the king and Dylan pulled out both golden apples. He then pulled off his clothes and under them was a shiny gold suit of armor and red cape. Dylan and the beautiful princess were married and his brothers did not laugh at him again!

The End

THE REAL PRINCESS (25)

The prince wanted to marry a princess - not just any princess, but a real princess. He traveled all over the country, but could never be sure that when a girl said she was a princess, that she would be a real princess. How could he tell for sure? Finally he gave up his search and returned home. "Mother, I cannot be sure that I have found any real princess. I will not settle for less," he said sorrowfully.

That night there was a terrible storm. The thunder and lightning raged. Then there was a tapping at the door. A servant opened the door and there stood a young girl! Her hair was dripping. Rain dripped from her nose and chin! Her clothes were soaking

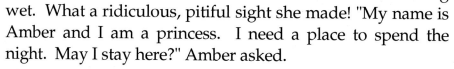
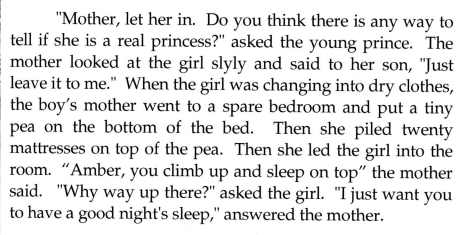

wet. What a ridiculous, pitiful sight she made! "My name is Amber and I am a princess. I need a place to spend the night. May I stay here?" Amber asked.

"Mother, let her in. Do you think there is any way to tell if she is a real princess?" asked the young prince. The mother looked at the girl slyly and said to her son, "Just leave it to me." When the girl was changing into dry clothes, the boy's mother went to a spare bedroom and put a tiny pea on the bottom of the bed. Then she piled twenty mattresses on top of the pea. Then she led the girl into the room. "Amber, you climb up and sleep on top" the mother said. "Why way up there?" asked the girl. "I just want you to have a good night's sleep," answered the mother.

Amber tried all night to sleep, but could not. She tossed and turned the whole night. In the morning the mother asked how she had slept. "Oh, it was the most dreadful night. I am black and blue all over. There must have been something awfully hard under my mattress," said the pretty princess.

So the queen went to her son and told him the girl was a real princess, or else she would not have felt the pea. Only a real princess could be so tender that a pea would hurt her when placed under twenty mattresses. So at last the prince found his real princess. He and Amber were married and lived happily ever after.

The End

128

THE SIX TRAVELERS (65)

One day a soldier was walking angrily down a road. On his discharge from the army he received only three farthings from the king. He was determined to get more money from the king. By and by he came upon a man so strong he was pulling up trees as though they were weeds. The soldier stopped and said, "I'm on my way to make a fortune. Come with me and we cannot fail." And the two set off together.

Presently they came upon another man who was aiming his rifle at something. They asked, "What are you shooting at?" The man replied, "I have great eyesight and I am just practicing. I'm going to shoot the right eye from the fly sitting in a tree two miles away." The soldiers asked this man to join them and he did.

Next they came upon a man who wore his hat over one ear. They all asked him why he wore his hat like this. "If I straightened my hat a great frost would come. My ear makes everything cold." "Oh, come with us! " they pleaded and he joined the three men.

Soon they came upon a man who was standing on one leg, holding the other. It was not attached to his body. They asked what he was doing. "I must take my leg off at times, for if I strap it on and use both legs, I go too fast. I am the fastest runner in the world." "Oh my! Why don't you travel with us! " they begged, and he joined them in their quest.

In a little while they came upon a man who was blowing air from one nostril. They asked him why he was doing that. "I am blowing a windmill which is three miles away. If I used both nostrils, I would blow it over." They asked him to come with them, and he agreed to go along.

They soon came to a town where they heard there was a contest going on. "The king is offering his daughter as a reward to any man who can run faster than her to a mountain stream and bring back a cup of water," a man told them. So they went to the king and the soldier asked if he could have his servant run for him. The king agreed to this, but said that if the servant lost, both he and the soldier would lose their heads! That did not worry them, and soon the race began.

The king's daughter was off like a flash, but in less than the blink of an eye, the runner had passed her up. He ran to the mountain stream, filled his cup with water and started back. He became tired and knowing he had plenty of time, he lay down to rest. In time the princess came by and saw the man sleeping. She emptied the water from his cup and ran on. But the man with the good eyes had seen what happened. He took out his rifle and shot a bullet so close to the sleeping man's head that he woke. He saw his cup was now empty and ran to refill it and still he passed up the princess and of course he won the race!

The princess and the king were not pleased that she should have to marry a common soldier and decided to be rid of them. They took the six men to a room, bolted the door from the outside and left. The king then ordered his servants to light a fire under the room, for the floor and walls were made of solid metal and they figured that after the fire made the room hot enough, the men would suffocate. Presently the room became hot. The men began to realize what was happening when they could not open the door, so the man took off his hat and put it on top of his head and the room immediately became cold.

When the king came back and saw this would not work, he said the soldier could have all the money he could carry if he would not marry the princess. The soldier agreed if his servant could carry it for him. Then he went to town and had a huge bag made. When the king had his servants bring gold to fill the bag, it took twenty of them to fill the bottom of the bag. The soldier demanded they bring more, and more and more and more. When it was finally filled, the strong man slung the bag over his shoulders as though it were only a bag of feathers.

As the six of them started off the king decided no one was going to take that much of his wealth. He sent his army after them. But when the six men saw the army coming after them, the fellow that had the strong nostrils just blew them all away - clear back to the king's castle. Then the six travelers went on their way in peace, to divide up all the money.

The End

THE SPINDLE, THE SHUTTLE, AND THE NEEDLE (44)

There was once a poor young girl who lived alone in a cottage. The girl made her living by spinning, weaving and sewing. She worked very hard, but still she was very poor.

Now the king had a son who was looking for a bride. He was not allowed to marry any girl that was poor, yet he did not like the rich girls. He swore to marry only a girl that was both poor and rich. He went to the nearest village and asked who the richest girl was. The people told him and he went to see her. She was sitting idly in her rich clothes doing nothing at all. He said not one word to her but rode on.

At the next village he asked who was the poorest girl in the village and was told of the girl that made her living by spinning, weaving and sewing. He went to her cottage and peeked through the window. She was not sitting idly, but was working hard at her spindle. The girl glanced up and saw the prince. She did not know who he was but smiled at him and kept on working. The prince left her, too, without a word, but thought of the beautiful girl on his way. It was too bad the girl could not be rich, as well as poor! The girl continued with her work, but her thoughts turned to the man that had peeked through the window. How handsome he was! Then she sang:

"Spindle, spindle, out with you, bring me home a lover true."

Suddenly her spindle leaped away and skipped out the house trailing a golden thread behind it! The girl ran after it, but it ran so merrily along that she could not catch it. She gave up and went back to her cottage. She sat down at her shuttle and began working and singing:

"Shuttle, shuttle, weave some more, a pretty carpet for my floor."

Right away the shuttle pulled away from the girl! It ran to the doorstep and began weaving the most beautiful carpet! The girl went to her sewing and started singing again:

"Needle, needle, sharp and fine, fit the house for lover mine."

The needle jumped from her hand and ran about the room. It quickly made covers for the chairs and curtains for the windows. Such a pretty, rich looking room it was, especially with the new carpet.

The prince had followed the thread all the way back to the cottage of the poor girl. When he entered and saw the poor maiden in the rich looking room, he at once knew this was the girl he was looking for. "You are both the poorest and the richest girl. Please come and be my bride." She blushed and smiled at the handsome prince and promised to be true to him always. The prince married her and she never again was poor. The spindle, the shuttle and the needle were put in a safe place where the prince and the princess could always look at them and cherish them.

The End

THE STORY OF THE BAT ((30)

War had been declared! The birds against the beasts, and the beasts against the birds! As both armies lined up in preparation for battle, a small creature hovered overhead. He flew down to the army of beasts. "What are you?" the beast leader asked. "I am a beast, and I am called a bat. I have fur on my body and four legs and teeth. No matter that I can fly, I am still a beast!" he cried. So the beasts let him join them. After a day of battle it looked like the beasts might lose, so the bat flew off quietly to the army of birds. "What are you?" the bird leader asked. "I am a bird, and I am called a bat. See me fly!" He did fly, so the birds invited him to fight with them.

Soon the birds were losing and the bat decided to go back to the beasts. As he neared the beasts, the lion yelled, "Where have you been? Are you a spy for the birds?" "Oh, no. I flew over there to see how things were doing. They are losing and we will beat them easily," said the bat, and he fought with the beasts again.

It wasn't long before the beasts were losing again and the bat thought he would do better to get back on the birds' side again. As he started back two of the sentries that had been posted saw him coming. They grabbed him and accused him of spying on them for the beasts. "Oh, no, I only flew over there to see how they were doing. We are going to beat them easily," said the bat.

Yes, the beasts were losing again. The birds started bringing in some of the beasts as war prisoners. The beasts, thinking the bat was really on their side hailed him. "So they got you, too?" yelled one of the beasts. "What do you mean, got you, too? He is a bird and he fights with us," said one of the birds.

Well, the birds and the beasts called a treaty so they could discuss this creature who called himself a bird one time and a beast another. No one cares for a traitor so they sentenced him from that day on that he would neither be a bird, nor a beast. He would have to fly only at night and hang by his claw during the day in some dark, out of the way place. He would always remain only half a bird, and half a beast. The birds and beasts would be friends with each other and the bat would never be a friend of either.

The End

THE STRAW, THE COAL AND THE BEAN (16)

One day an old woman was going to boil some beans for her lunch. She gathered some straw and coal and set it to burning under the pot. Then she poured in the beans. One of the beans fell to the floor beside a piece of straw. "Whew! I sure was lucky to escape from that boiling water!" said the bean to the straw. "I was really lucky to escape from the fire!" said the straw. About that time a hot coal rolled from the fire over next to the straw and the bean. "Goodness, did you see that! I could have been burned to ashes!"

yelped the coal. "We have really had a stroke of good fortune," said the straw. "Well, let's just stick together and get out of here before we are found!" yelled the bean. And they all skipped out the door together.

They went out into the country and soon came to a small stream. "How do we get across?" whimpered the coal. "I will lay myself down across the stream and you two can walk across on my back," said the straw. "Oh, what a good idea. I'll go first, said the coal. He jumped onto the straw and started across. When he got to the middle of the stream he became frightened and found he could not go a step further. "Hurry, you're going to burn me in half!" yelled the straw. "I can't go on. I'm scared!" yelled the frightened coal. Finally the straw burnt in half and the straw and the coal both fell into the water!

Meanwhile, the pretty white bean had been sitting cautiously on the bank. He thought the whole matter very funny and began to laugh! He laughed and laughed until finally his sides split! "Oh, look at my pretty white coat," he moaned.

A tailor had been sitting nearby watching. He went over to the bean and sewed him up. But the only thread he had was black, so the white bean ended up with a black seam. And that is why, to this day, some beans have black seams.

The End

THE TABLE, THE DONKEY AND THE STICK (34)

There once was a man who had three sons. He told each son they must go into the world and learn to earn their own way. The first boy hired himself out to a carpenter. After he had worked a full year and knew the trade well, the carpenter paid him his wages by giving him a table. "When you want food, just say, `Spread, table,' and the table will spread a fine meal upon itself," said the carpenter. The boy thanked the carpenter and started for home. He stopped to spend the night at an inn for he was a long way from home yet. Upon entering the inn the innkeeper said he did not have enough food to serve him. "That is all right," said the boy. "Sit down at my table and we will have a fine meal." The innkeeper sat down and the boy said, "Spread, table!" and the table spread itself with a fine meal!

That night, the innkeeper waited for the boy to go to sleep and then he exchanged one of his own tables for the magic table. The boy didn't know the difference and took the wrong table home. When he tried to show his father what the table could do, he

found that the table did nothing. He decided the table had only been good for one time, so he dropped the matter and took up his trade as a carpenter.

The second boy hired himself out to a cooper. In a year he had learned to make fine barrels. The cooper paid him his wages with a donkey. "This is a magic donkey. When you want gold, just pull the donkey's tail and say, 'Spit gold,' and it will spit out a mouthful of gold." The boy thanked the man and headed home. This boy also stopped at the same inn. When he put his donkey in the stable the innkeeper saw the boy pull the donkey's tail and say, "Spit gold," and it spit out gold pieces. So that night, when the boy was sleeping, the innkeeper exchanged the magic donkey with a worthless donkey. On arriving home, the boy found his donkey would no longer spit gold. No matter how many times he pulled his tail the donkey only kicked him! He decided he should have had the donkey spit out more gold at the inn, for he very probably would never get any more!

The third son had hired himself out to a miller. It took him just over a year to learn to bake bread and cookies well enough to go home and make his living. The miller gave the boy a stick as his year's wages. "All you must do is say, 'Stick, beat!' and it will beat anyone who has wronged you," said the miller.

The boy took his stick and headed for home. He had received a letter from his brothers that explained they had also received magic things, but had lost them along the way. They had both spent the night at the same inn. They begged their brother that if he should receive any magic thing to bring it straight home and not to stop at any inn, for the thing might lose its magic the first time it was used, as theirs had.

The boy walked a long way and became very tired. He could not find another place to spend the night so he stopped at the very inn that his brothers had stopped. When he ordered his meal, the innkeeper, instead of preparing the food simply said, "Spread table" and his table was spread with food! Now the boy knew his brothers were right. What should he do?

The boy innocently asked the innkeeper if he had a donkey to sell. "I have only one donkey, and he is very definitely not for sale!" laughed the innkeeper.

Thereupon, the boy yelled, "Stick, beat!" and the stick began to beat upon the innkeeper. The stick chased the man around the room until the man was yelling, "Make it stop!" But the boy did not make the stick stop until he had the truth from the innkeeper. The innkeeper did not like giving him the table and the donkey, but he also did not like being beat upon by the stick!

When the third son arrived home with the table, the donkey and the stick, they had quite a party! They invited all their neighbors and had the table spread food for all. They had the donkey spit out enough gold for everyone so that no one in the town was left poor. And they never had to worry about anyone stealing the table or donkey for they made sure to tell everyone about their magic stick!

The End

THE TALE OF THE YOUTH WHO SET OUT TO LEARN WHAT FEAR WAS (35)

A father had two sons, the oldest was very clever, but the younger was stupid. All he talked about was learning how to shudder. "Everyone knows how to shudder but me," he whimpered. One day his father came to him and said he must learn to do something with his life so he could make his own way in the world. "But first I must learn to shudder," said the boy. The tired father said, "All right, if you must learn, the minister at the church said he would teach you. Go to him."

The youth asked the minister, "Sir, can you really teach me to shudder?" The minister said, "Yes, just go up the steps to the attic." After the lad went up the steps, the minister secretly went up behind him. He pulled a sheet over his head and stood where the lad could see him. "Who's there?" asked the lad. No answer. "I asked who's there? Either tell me or I shall knock you down!" yelled the youth. No answer. After yelling one more time for the thing to reveal itself, he knocked it down the stairs!

Upon arriving at the minister's home the wife asked where her husband was. "Oh, no. I hope he was not the foolish thing I knocked down the stairs!" whimpered the youth. They ran to the church and there lay the minister with a broken leg. "Leave us!" yelled the minister. "You have no fear and I cannot teach you to shudder."

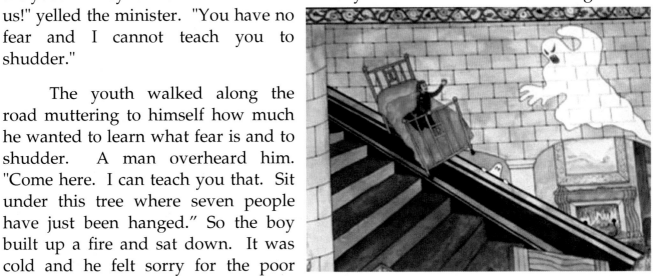

The youth walked along the road muttering to himself how much he wanted to learn what fear is and to shudder. A man overheard him. "Come here. I can teach you that. Sit under this tree where seven people have just been hanged." So the boy built up a fire and sat down. It was cold and he felt sorry for the poor bodies hanging above. He climbed the tree and took them down and sat the bodies by the fire. But the dead bodies just sat there so still that the sparks flew about and caught their clothes on fire. Thinking they must be warm now, he knocked out the fire and hung them back up in the tree.

The next morning when the man came back and found the boy had learned nothing, he said, "I know of a haunted castle. The king will let anyone who can spend three nights in it alone, marry his beautiful daughter. You can surely learn what fear is and to shudder in a haunted castle." So the youth went to the king and explained his problem. The king decided to let the youth have a try. He was told he could take three things with him and the boy chose a lathe, a bench and a knife. Then he set out to spend the three nights alone in the castle.

That evening the young lay down on a bed. Then the bed started to move around. Then it flew all around the room! "Oh what fun! Whee!" yelled the boy. The bed flew faster and faster until it suddenly halted and turned upside down on the boy. The youth laughed and climbed out from under the bed. He lay down by the fire knowing he could never get any sleep on that bed.

The second night as he was sitting quietly, half a man dropped down from the chimney. A moment later another half dropped down. Then more men started dropping all around. They picked up nine skeleton legs and a skull and started to bowl with them. "If I put those skulls on my lathe and make them round for you, can I play?" asked the youth. They agreed and they all had a great game.

The third night six men came in with a coffin. They placed it beside him and left. The boy took the lid off the coffin and there was a dead corpse. "My, how cold you are you poor thing," said the youth. He started rubbing the corpse's hands but the corpse would not warm up. Then he climbed into the coffin. "When two people lay together their bodies warm each other so I will warm you up!" he smiled. Soon the body stirred and sat up. It grabbed the youth by the neck and tried to choke him. The youth jumped out and slammed the lid shut. "What gratitude," he mumbled to himself.

Suddenly a monster appeared. It looked a lot like a man with a long beard, but was too big and ugly to be only a man. "I am the strongest thing alive, and I am going to kill you!" shouted the monster. "Oh, I don't know. I am pretty strong myself," said the youth. "Come with me and we shall see who is the strongest," said the monster. He led the youth into a forging room. He picked up an anvil and broke it in half! "Oh, that wasn't much," laughed the boy. "Watch me closely," said the boy. As the monster drew near to watch, the youth seized his knife and killed it!

The next morning the king came. "Well, are you now fearful and have you learned to shudder?" laughed the king. But the boy shook his head sadly. "Well, at any rate, you have earned my daughter in marriage," said the king.

The youth and his wife were happy together but he still muttered about not being able to shudder. The wife tired of this muttering and decided she would teach him to shudder herself. One night while he was sleeping she went to the stream and filled her pail with dozens of little fishes. She went back to her sleeping husband and poured the whole pail of little fishes on him. They swam all about through his clothes. He awoke and cried, "Stop, stop, dear wife! Now I know what shuddering is!"

The End

THE TERRIBLE HEAD (72)

There was once a king that had been told by a sorceress that his own grandson would one day kill him, so to keep his daughter from ever having a child, the king had a pit dug and put his daughter into it. The princess sat in the pit for many days and thought she would never get out. One day as she lay weeping, the sky showered golden dust upon her and soon after the princess had a baby boy. The king, terrified, had a small boat built and put his daughter and his new baby grandson in it and had it floated out to the sea. The little boat drifted awhile and came to rest in a new country. A kind man walking by found the boat, the princess and her baby boy and he took them home and let them live with him.

When the boy had grown nearly to manhood, the king of their new country desired to marry the boy's mother. Knowing she would never part with her boy, and not wanting the boy to come live with him, he made a plan to be rid of the boy. He told the boy a great queen was to be married and every person must come and bring a rich gift. "But I have no money to buy a rich gift," said the boy. "Well, if you have no money, perhaps you could bring `The Terrible Head' for a gift" laughed the king. "If a living man can do it, I can and I will!" bragged the boy. "Just tell me where to find this Head."

So the king told him that a long way off were three sisters. They had claws of brass and rather than hair, had serpents on their heads. Anyone who looked upon their faces turned to stone. The youngest had strange eyes and she was the only one that could be killed of the three. She was the one with The Terrible Head.

The boy thought for a long time. How could he find this place with The Terrible Head. And if he did, why would he not also turn to stone? Suddenly a tall and strange man appeared. "What is troubling you, young man?" asked the strange man. The boy told him his problem about The Terrible Head. This strange man had the perfect answer. All he had to do was put on these magic flying shoes that he wore. They would fly him to the Three Grey Brothers where he would be told how to get the Cap of Darkness and the Sword of Sharpness that he would need.

The boy put on the shoes and they flew him over the seas and mountains and towns - straight to the Three Gray Brothers. They were so old that none of them had any eyes, only empty sockets. They had one good eye which they were passing back and forth so they each could take a turn seeing. The first brother was passing the eye to another when the boy stepped between them and grabbed it. "Where is the eye, Brother?" "Why I just passed it to you!" said the first brother. "No. I have it!" cried the boy. "And I will not give it back until you tell me how to find the Cap of Darkness and the Sword of Sharpness so I may go get The Terrible Head. Will you tell me or shall I keep your eye?"

"You will first have to go to The Fairies of the Garden. They have the Cap of Darkness and the Sword of Sharpness and will show you the way from there. To get there, go north over four mountains and three rivers and one town. Now, please give us back the eye," said the third brother.

When he arrived at the land of The Fairies of the Garden, he was excited that he might soon accomplish this terrible mission. The garden had three dancing fairies in it and they gave him the much needed Sword of Sharpness and the Cap of Darkness. They put the Cap of Darkness on his head and told him he was now invisible even to them! Then they gave him a bag and a shield that was as shiny as a mirror and told him the way to The Terrible Head.

His flying shoes took him the way they had said. From above he could see the three horrible looking women sleeping on the ground by the river. He dropped to the ground beside them and turned his back. By looking into his shiny shield it served as a mirror. In this way he would not have to look directly on them--that would mean turning to stone and instant death. The two ugly ones were sleeping with their heads tucked under their wings. The youngest one was sleeping face up, though with her eyes wide open! By looking in his shiny shield, with one quick blow, he struck off The Terrible Head with his Sword of Sharpness. He grabbed it up and pushed it into the bag and flew away faster than the wind. The two ugly sisters woke at once and took chase, but since they could not see him with his Cap of Darkness, they soon lost him.

Flying above a river on his way home, he looked down and saw a beautiful girl chained to a tree. He flew down and cut off the chain with his Sword of Sharpness. Knowing the girl could not see him, he took off the Cap of Darkness. She began weeping. "Are you here to save me from the monster in the sea?" she asked. "What monster?" he asked. At that very instant, a monster rose out of the sea. The boy pulled The Terrible Head out of his bag and held it up for the monster to see. As promised, the monster turned to stone! The girl then told him how each day a girl was offered as food for the monster so it would not come on land to hunt for food. This day, she had been chosen as the one to be eaten. She was a king's daughter and her father would reward him greatly if he would just take her home! The king rejoiced when he saw his daughter was saved and granted the boy any wish he wanted. The boy thought her the most beautiful girl on the earth and asked to marry her and they were married right away and stayed with her

140

father a short time, but soon the boy decided he must do as he had set out to do, return to his home with The Terrible Head.

When they arrived at the boy's town, the first person he saw was his very own mother. She was running from the very king that had demanded he go after The Terrible Head. The king was out to kill the poor woman because she refused to marry him. Now the boy pulled forth The Terrible Head and cried "Here it is, the head I promised you!" The king looked at The Head and turned to stone. All the people of the town threw a big party to celebrate the death of the wicked king. They appointed a new king who was the good and kind man who had raised the boy.

The boy and his mother longed to return to their country of birth. When they arrived in their home country, there was a contest going on giving prizes to the best runners, jumpers, and iron ring throwers. The boy thought it looked like fun. "I must try the iron ring throwing." He threw the iron ring so hard and so far that it went into the crowd. It struck a man on the head and he died right where he was standing. When it was inquired who the man was, the boy found that it was his own grandfather, the king who had been so frightened that his grandson would one day kill him that he had flown from his throne and had been posing as a servant. Thus, the prophecy was fulfilled that the grandson would kill the king.

The End

THE THREE BEARS (58)

One morning the three bears sat down to their breakfast of hot porridge. "Oh, my porridge is too hot!" said Baby Bear. "Let's go for a walk in the woods while it cools," said Papa. And off they went for a short walk in the woods.

Goldilocks was taking a walk in the woods, too. She came upon the bears' house and wondered who lived there. She knocked at the door and it opened, but nobody was home. The most delicious smell came drifting toward her. Gee, she must have a taste of that! She tried Papa Bear's porridge but it was just too hot! Then she tried Mama Bear's porridge and ugh, it was too cold! Then she tried Baby Bear's porridge and it was just right, and she ate it all up!

She wandered through the house and saw three chairs in the parlor. She went to the biggest one which was Papa Bear's chair and climbed up into it. "My, this is too high. I can't see over the sides!" She went to the next one but it was very lumpy and uncomfortable. "Well, still one more I can try." She went to sit in Baby Bear's chair.

"Oh, good, this is just right!" she said. But she had no sooner said that than CRASH! It broke! She was too big to sit in that little chair.

She strolled on around the house and into the bedroom. By now Goldilocks had completely forgotten about being in a stranger's house. She was so tired! She climbed up into the biggest bed. "Oh, my, how hard this bed is. I'll try the next one," she mumbled to herself, but the second bed was too soft. It was not comfortable at all to have the mattress squishing up on all sides of her! "Guess I'll try the little one," she said to no one in particular. It was just perfect! She lay there and was soon sound asleep.

By now the three bears had tired of their walk and were just coming in the door. They immediately went to their porridge. "Someone has been eating my porridge!" said Papa Bear. "Why, someone has been eating mine, too!" said Mama Bear. "Well, whoever was eating your porridge must have been awfully hungry. They ate mine all up!" whimpered poor Baby Bear.

Papa Bear went looking through the house for the intruder. "Come see this. Someone has been sitting in my chair!" he yelled. "Someone has been sitting in mine, too," said Mama Bear. "Well, they not only sat in mine, but broke it!" cried Baby Bear.

Papa Bear stormed on through the house! He ran into the bedroom. "Come look at this!" he screamed. "Someone has been in my bed!" "Mine, too!" said Mama Bear. "Oh, look, look!" screamed Baby Bear. "Here is the person who ate all my porridge, broke my chair and is now sleeping in my bed!! Who do you think you are?" he screamed at Goldilocks.

Goldilocks woke up and sat straight up in the tiny bed. BEARS! She didn't wait around to answer any questions but ran straight out of the house and straight home! BEARS! My gracious, she would never walk into a stranger's house again.

The End

THE THREE BILLY GOATS GRUFF, A FABLE (26)

The three Billy Goats Gruff were on their way to the other side of the stream to eat some tall, green grass. They had to cross the bridge that the old mean Troll lived under and was always trying to catch and eat them but today they had a good plan. They were bringing their bigger and older brother with them.

The smallest billy goat started across. "Click, clack, click, clack," went the bridge. "Who's crossing my bridge?" yelled the Troll. "Oh, it is only I, little bitty Billy Goat Gruff," he squeaked in his small voice. "I need to cross the bridge so I can reach the other side and make myself big and fat." "Don't worry about making yourself fat, for I am going to eat you up!" yelled the Troll. "Oh, don't bother with me, I am too small. Wait till my brother comes across. He is much bigger than I," said the little billy goat. "Well, run on then so I can get a bigger meal," yelled the old Troll.

Then the second billy goat, who was much bigger, started across. "Clack, conk, clack, conk," went the bridge. "Who is crossing over my bridge?" yelled the Troll. "Just me," the second billy goat said. "Well, I am going to eat you up!" yelled the Troll. "Don't bother with me, wait till my bigger brother billy goat comes across because he is much fatter," said the second billy goat. "Well, run on then, so I can get a bigger meal," yelled the old mean Troll.

Then the biggest billy goat you have ever seen started across. "Conk, clunk, conk, clunk!" went the bridge under his heavy weight. "Who's crossing my bridge?" yelled the old Troll. "It is I, Big Billy Goat Gruff - what's it to you?" roared the biggest billy goat. "I am going to eat you, that's what!" yelled the Troll. "Well, you just come up here and try!" roared the huge goat. So the Troll climbed up and they charged at each other. Big Billy Goat Gruff ran the Troll through with his horns and killed him! For ever after, the goats were free to use the bridge and needn't worry about that mean old Troll who thought the bridge should just belong to him.

The End

Moral: Sometimes you just use your wits to obtain a goal. Sometimes it takes strength.

THE THREE LITTLE PIGS (57)

The three little pigs had always lived with their mother. One day their mother decided they were all old enough to be on their own. She handed each of them a small amount of money and told them to go into the world, build your houses and take care of each other. "Just always remember to be on the watch for the mean old wolf," she warned.

The first little pig was a good little pig, but very, very lazy. He was in a hurry to build his house so he could have time to play. He found some straw by the road, picked it up and built his house out of straw. He still had his money and lots of time to play.

The second little pig was also a little bit lazy, but a little bit smarter. He knew a stick house was stronger than straw, so he went into town and bought a bunch of sticks with half his money. He still had half his money left and it didn't take long to build a stick house.

The third little pig was a very hard worker and very smart. He wanted a good strong house, so he went to town and used all his money to pay for a load of bricks. He had no money left, and it took a lot of hard work to build his brick house, but he knew it would be strong and safe.

The mean old wolf had been watching the three little pigs. "Here goes three easy dinners for me!" he thought to himself. He ran over to the first little pig's straw house. "Little pig, little pig, let me in," he yelled. "No, I won't let you in!" cried the little pig.

"Then I'll huff and puff and blow your straw house down!" yelled the wolf, and he did! As the straw blew into the air, the pig ran for safety to his second brother's house of sticks.

The wolf chased him all the way there. "Little pigs, little pigs, let me in!" yelled the wolf. "No, no!" cried the two little pigs. "Well, then I'll huff and puff and blow your stick house down," snarled the wolf, and he did! Well the sticks fell all over the wolf and the two little pigs ran straight to their brother's brick house with the wolf right behind them!

Now the wolf was getting mad. He knew this house of bricks was going to be hard to blow down, but he wasn't going to give up yet. "Little pigs, little pigs, please let me in," said the wolf. "No, we won't." they all cried together. "Well, then I'll huff and puff and blow this house down!" screamed the mean old wolf. He blew himself up really big. Then he huffed and he puffed and he huffed and puffed, but he could not blow a brick house down! He went away very angry.

That evening the wolf came back. "Little pigs," called the wolf very sweetly, "let's be friends. Meet me at Farmer Joe's house in the morning at 6:00 and we'll all pick some apples and make something good to eat." Oh, boy did that wolf have a plan! "O.K.," said the third pig, and he made plans, too.

The next morning, at 5:00 the pigs went to Farmer Joe's house and picked apples before the wolf was to be there. On their way home they saw him coming. "Oh, dear, what do we do now?" cried the two lazy pigs. The third pig grabbed a barrel and emptied out the apples. "Jump in!" he yelled. They all hopped into the barrel and it rolled down the hill, right over the wolf and down to the brick house. They jumped out of the barrel and scrambled through the door and into the brick house.

Now, the wolf didn't like that at all! He was determined to eat them! He climbed up on the roof of the brick house and yelled down the chimney, "Here I come. You won't get away this time!"

The three little pigs had put a pot of water on to boil before they left home so they could cook their apples when they got them home. When that mean old wolf jumped down the chimney, he landed right in the pot of boiling water - and that was the end of the mean old wolf!

The End

THE THREE WISHES (13)

One day a woodsman was walking through the woods. He went up to a tree and examined it. "Oh, this tree would be a good tree to cut down and use for firewood," he said out loud.

"Oh, no, please do not cut this tree down," said a very small voice. "Who's there?" asked the woodsman. "I don't see anyone!" Then the little voice said, "You can't see me. I am a wood fairy and I live in this tree. If you will save this tree and not cut it down, you may have three wishes - anything you want!" The woodsman left the tree alone and ran home to tell his wife all about the fairy and the three wishes they had now.

The wife set a bowl of porridge before him. He frowned and said, "What is this porridge for? This is all we ever have. I wish I had a big sausage to eat!" And at those words, the porridge disappeared and a big sausage was lying before him on the table!

The wife got very angry at that! "You stupid man, we only have three wishes and you go and waste one wishing for a stupid sausage. Haven't you any sense? I wish that sausage was hanging from your stupid nose!" And at those words, the sausage jumped up and stuck on the woodsman's nose!

Now the woodsman was angry! He pulled and tugged and tried to cut it off, but it was a magic sausage, and nobody was going to get it off! "That's all right, Dear," said the wife. "Nobody will ever notice it but you. We'll be so rich that people will be looking at all we have, not at your nose.

The woodsman was really angry now. "I can't go around with a sausage hanging from my nose all my life, no matter how rich we are. I wish this stupid sausage had never been mentioned, let alone stuck on my nose!" he cried. And with those words, the sausage disappeared, and the woodsman and his wife were left sitting there staring at each other!

The End

THE TINDER BOX (84)

A soldier had been away at war and was walking home and thinking about how he could make his fortune. He came upon a lady in a red dress and black cape. "Soldier, come here!" said the lady. "I will make you a rich man if you will do me a favor. Climb up into the hole in that tree and I will lower you down where you will find three rooms, three dogs and a fortune in coins which you may keep. All I ask is that you bring me the tinder box that you will find in the last room. When you want to come back up, yell and I will pull you up with this rope."

Why not? This was a fast way to make a fortune, so the soldier tied the rope around his waist, climbed up the tree, squeezed through the hole and the lady lowered him down into a great hall. In the first room there sat a dog beside a sack of copper pieces. He grabbed the sack went to the second room. In this room he found a bigger dog and a sack of silver pieces. He grabbed that sack and headed for the next room. In the third room he found another large dog, the tinder box which had a small candle, some matches and a sack of gold pieces.

He grabbed it all and called to the lady to pull him up. "Why don't you want any of the gold?" he asked her. She laughed at him and said the gold would vanish if he did not have the tinder box. Well, that was no good! So he knocked her down and ran off with all the money and the tinder box!

The soldier bought a fine house and gave many parties. He had many friends now and they all sat around and talked about the princess that lived in the nearby castle. It was said the queen had been told by a fortune teller that her daughter would one day marry a common soldier, so the queen kept her daughter locked in her room so she would never meet the common soldier. The soldier laughed at the story and continued partying and spending his silver and gold pieces wastefully. Finally he ran out of money and had to move out of the fine house and rent a small room. Eventually he didn't have money for food and finally even ran out of candles to light his small room. Then he remembered the tinder box had a tiny candle in it. He pulled out the candle and struck one of the matches against the tinder box to light it. As soon as he struck the box the first dog from the first room appeared! "What do you command?" asked the dog. My goodness! No wonder the old lady wanted the tinder box! He told the dog to fetch him a bag full of money. No sooner said, than done!

148

When he struck the box again, the second, bigger dog appeared. So he struck it three times and there stood the third and biggest dog. Each asked what he commanded, and he commanded them to bring him more money, and they did! Now the soldier moved back into his fine house and started giving parties again but found himself terribly lonely at times. He often dreamed of the princess in the nearby castle and longed to see her. Such a lonely thing she must be locked in her room. So he called the biggest dog to him and told the dog to go and fetch the princess. In the blink of an eye the dog was back with the princess sound asleep on its back. She was so beautiful and he kissed her cheek! He had the dog take her back without ever waking her.

The next day the princess told the queen that she had dreamed of a dog taking her to a soldier who had kissed her. The queen wanted to make certain it was a dream and had not really happened. She filled a small bag with flour, cut a small hole in the bag and tied the bag to her daughter's nightgown. That night when the soldier sent the dog to get the princess, the flour spilled from the little bag, making a trail all the way to the soldier's house and back to the princess' castle. The very next day the soldier was arrested and thrown into prison.

Now what? He surely wished he had his tinder box and his dogs now to help him. He leaned out the prison window and yelled to a small boy. "Little boy, go and get the tinder box from my house and bring it to me and I will reward you." The boy was off at once and soon brought the tinder box back to the soldier.

When the guards came to take the prisoner before the king, the soldier struck the tinder box three times and all three dogs appeared! The dogs ran at the king as the soldier told them to. "Stop the dogs!" yelled the king. "Only if you give me my freedom and let me marry the princess!" cried the soldier. So the king granted the soldier his freedom and said he could marry the princess and the soldier called off the dogs. The next day the soldier and the princess were married. The three dogs all joined in the wedding feast and ate as much ham and chicken as they wanted!

The End

THE TWELVE DANCING PRINCESSES (33)

Once there was a king with twelve daughters. The king loved them all very much and each night he locked them in their room to make sure no harm could come to them. But, each morning when the king went to unlock their door he found that each of the girls needed new shoes! He could not understand what could be happening. It was as though they must be dancing all night, every night. How could this be?

At last the king issued a proclamation saying that any man could marry his choice of his daughters if he could find out why the princesses always needed new shoes. Young men came from all over the land. Every man wanted to have his choice of the lovely girls. But every morning, none were able to tell the king anything, for every young man fell asleep during the night.

One day an older soldier heard of this and thought he might have a chance. On his way to the castle he came upon an old woman who was hungry and asked for food. "I will gladly share what little bit of food I have with you," said the kind soldier. The woman ate the food and thanked him. "What can I do to repay you?" asked the woman. He laughed and said all he wished was that someone could help him catch the twelve princesses dancing. "That is easy enough," said the woman. "Just do not drink the water they will bring you at bedtime, for it would put you to sleep." Then she gave the soldier a cloak and told him it would make him invisible.

The soldier went to the king, but the king thought if the young men could not stay awake through the night, how could this older soldier? Still, he took him to his daughters' room and told him to sit in a chair where he could rest while he watched. When the king left, the eldest daughter came to the soldier and gave him a cup of water, but when she went away, the soldier threw the water out the window. Then he pretended to sleep.

Soon he heard them. "The water I gave him will keep him sleeping all night. Let's go now." He heard them putting on their shoes. They knocked on the wall and a secret door opened. The princesses hurried out. The soldier slipped on the magic cloak to make him invisible and went after them so fast that he stepped on the dress of the last girl on the stairway. "Someone stepped on my dress!" cried the girl. Her sisters called her silly and told her no one was behind her.

At the bottom of the stairway was a beautiful forest with trees that had leaves of silver and gold. The soldier picked a leaf from each kind of tree so he would have proof of being there. At last they came out of the forest and there was a lake with twelve boats and a prince in each boat. Each of the twelve girls went to a different boat. The soldier jumped into the last boat to leave and the last girl cried, "Someone got on the boat with me!" Again her sisters assured her no one was there.

They rowed across the lake and came to a castle. The princes and princesses jumped out and ran into the castle where musicians were playing loudly and they all started dancing. They danced the whole night. The old soldier even danced around by himself wishing he could fling off his invisible cloak and dance with the girls, but he did not. When it was nearly morning their shoes began wearing out, the girls stopped dancing. It was time to go back. The old soldier hopped into one of the boats and when they reached the shore he ran up the stairs ahead of the girls, threw off his coat and pretended to be sleeping soundly when they came in.

The next morning the soldier told the king what had happened. He showed the king the twigs of silver and gold. The king found this all hard to believe but called his daughters to him and asked them if it was true and they all admitted it was true.

The king asked the old soldier which daughter he wanted for a wife. "They are all beautiful, but they are all so young. I would prefer you let them marry the twelve princes. That would be payment enough for me to see them all happily married so that they could dance freely every night with their husbands," said the soldier. The king granted this wish and asked the old soldier to stay and live in the castle so he would never want for anything for the rest of his life. The soldier agreed to stay and from that night on, he danced with all the princesses and their husbands.

The End

THE UGLY DUCKLING (54)

A Mother Duck had been sitting on her nest of eggs for a long time. Suddenly the eggs started moving. She jumped up and watched the eggs hatch, all but one, the biggest one of all did not hatch. She sat back down and watched all her other pretty children quacking, swimming and playing. Finally the big egg started moving. She jumped up to watch her last child being born. The first thing she saw was a small dark head. Oh how ugly he was! Not at all like her other pretty ducklings.

One of the other mother ducks walked over. "My, what is that?" she asked. "That's my child," quacked his mother. "Well, I've never seen such an ugly thing. He probably isn't even a duckling at all, but a stupid turkey or something just as bad," she laughed and walked off.

That seemed to be the general opinion of the whole pond. If he wasn't a turkey, he was surely something just as bad, because he surely didn't look like the rest of the ducks. Even his own brothers and sisters wouldn't play with him. They laughed at him and told him to stay away from them.

"You children stop talking to your brother like that. Ugly is very sweet, even if he does not look quite as pretty as you," said their mother. "Oh, Mother," squeaked poor Ugly, "Nobody likes me. I can't even quack like the others, even though I can swim as well. I can't live among such unfriendly ducks." And he left to find a better world.

Ugly swam all around the big lake when he met up with some wild ducks. They asked what he was and he told them he must be a distant cousin of theirs, for he was a duck. They were friendly to him. "You are a bit ugly, but if you are a distant cousin you can stay with us," said one of the wild ducks. Suddenly shots rang out, over and over again. All around Ugly lay the dead ducks. Retriever dogs ran to pick up the dead ducks, but they didn't even touch Ugly. Such a small easy catch, too. It made him sad. He must really be ugly.

Ugly soon learned to fly. He would fly for a while and then stop and swim, but he was always chased away. He just didn't look like the other ducks and none of the ducks would play with him. Winter was coming and he didn't know where to go. Most ducks seemed to be flying south, but Ugly knew he would not be welcome to join them. Ice began to form on the pond and Ugly had to swim all day to keep enough water melted to swim in. The hole became smaller and smaller till he soon was spending all his time paddling his feet to keep it from freezing over. After a time he got so tired that he felt asleep. When he woke up his feet were frozen in the water. "Help!" he cried, "Help!"

A farmer passed by and heard his cry. He helped poor Ugly out and took him home to his children for a pet. Ugly had been mistreated so often that the children frightened him. He flew about the kitchen terrified. He flew straight into the milk pitcher and knocked the milk all over him. Then he flew into the flour bin and came out looking like a gob of paste! He saw an open window and flew out.

Ugly spent the rest of the winter alone. Needless to say, he had a very sad and lonely winter. But, at last spring came. Ugly was flying over a pond one day and saw a group of lovely swans. "Oh, to look as lovely as them!" he thought. The swans cried a greeting to him. "EEEEEEEEE" He cried back "EEEEEEEEE" to them. "Why he sounded just like a swan! He flew down and swam about the pond. When he looked into the mirror-like water, he couldn't believe his eyes. HE WAS A SWAN! No wonder he had never looked like the ducks. He was a swan himself, one of the most beautiful birds alive! No one would ever call him Ugly again.

The End

THE WILD SWANS (74)

There was once a king with 11 sons and 1 daughter, Elisia. Their mother had been dead for many years and the king remarried. Some people said the new wife was mean, but others said she was a witch! At first the children were delighted to have a new mother, but it turned out that their stepmother really was a witch! She talked their father into sending them away. Elisia, the only daughter, was sent to live with a nearby family. As the boys were leaving to find new homes, their stepmother followed them out. She put a curse on the brothers and changed them into wild swans! From then on they would spend all their days as swans and all their nights as humans. They would only be allowed to come to their homeland one night each year. The 11 swans flew off and made their new home in a faraway place. They missed their sister, but had no way to find her.

After a few years Elisia was allowed to return home. She came home a very beautiful, kind, and sweet woman. The stepmother was very angry and did not want the king to see the beautiful daughter and want her to stay. Before she took Sheila to see the king, she rubbed walnut juice over her body and mussed her hair. The king was disappointed to see his daughter return so dirty and messy and ordered her out of the house.

Poor Elisia had missed her father badly and now was ordered out of the house. She ran into the woods to cry. She took a bath in a stream and washed and fluffed her pretty hair. She hoped to find her brothers but did not know they were swans at all. She walked through the woods and came upon an old lady. "Have you seen 11 princes here in the woods?" she asked the lady. "No, but I saw 11 swans over by that small pond a few minutes ago," she said. At least she could hide behind a bush and watch the beautiful swans awhile. She sat watching them very quietly. As the sun disappeared, the swans suddenly turned into her brothers! Elisia ran to hug them. How badly they had all missed each other all these years. Now they could be together again.

Elisia's brothers told her the story about how their stepmother had put the curse upon them. Tomorrow they must return to their new home. "Take me with you," begged Elisia. They all agreed and set about making a net in which to carry her. When Elisia woke in the morning, she was being carried very gently in the net, high up in the sky, by her brothers, the 11 swans.

When the swans became men that night, they all sat around and talked. "Is there any way we can rid you of the curse?" asked Elisia. "No, not that we know of," they replied. That night while Elisia slept, a fairy spoke to her in a dream. "You may rid your brothers of their curse only one way. Gather the nettles that grow by the cave. Crush them and make it into thread. Then weave the thread into 11 coats and throw them over your brothers all at one time. But you must not speak one word until the coats are on them, or else they will die.

The next morning, Elisia started to work. She gathered the nettles, even though they pricked her fingers and made them bleed, but this was the only way to save her brothers. When the swans came back that evening and turned into men, Elisia could not utter a word. The brothers talked to each other and decided that Elisia must have a good reason for working so hard and not speaking.

One day while the swans were away, a prince came riding by. He saw Elisia working with the harsh nettles. He thought she must be living alone in the cave. "Come live with me at my castle and I will make you very happy," he begged her. She shook her head no, but she could not speak. The prince thought he should take her for her own good. She should not be living alone in a cave, especially when she could not even speak. So he captured her and took her to his castle. She will grow to love me and my castle the prince decided.

But Elisia was so unhappy. She missed seeing her brothers at night. And how could she ever complete the coats she had been making for them? She was not able to tell anyone of her worries.

As the days went by, the prince fell in love with Elisia and she, too, fell in love with the prince. Eventually they were married. Sometimes Elisia seemed happy, but other times she wept. She spoke to no one, ever. One day the prince surprised her and took her into a room that he had made to look just like the cave he had taken her from. He had even brought the coats she had been working on and they were lying there. Elisia was so happy! She started to work at once on the coats again.

Everyone at the castle loved Elisia except one man, the king's minister. He thought she must be a witch, for she was always sitting around working with the nettles and she never spoke. "She must be up to something evil," he said to the prince, but the prince only laughed at him. The minister started watching Elisia day and night. He would prove his point.

One night, Elisia ran out of nettles. She only had one coat left to be finished. She had seen some nettles growing not far from the castle. She tiptoed out of the castle hoping no one would stop her. But the minister saw her sneaking out into the night and he ran for the prince. "Oh, Prince, come see! She sneaks into the night alone. She is surely a witch and up to something evil!" The prince became worried. She had to be up to something evil to slink about so. The prince finally agreed that his wife must be tried as a witch.

The trial did not last long. They all agreed that Elisia was guilty of being a witch and sentenced her to prison! She spent her last night working on the last coat. If only she could get it done and get them on her brothers - but where were they? She had not seen them in months.

The swans had not seen their sister in months but they had been hunting for her. They looked high and low. They asked the birds around and finally found an old black crow who said their sister was married to a prince and was on trial for being a witch. That night the swans went to the palace and waited till just before daybreak. Then they went to the guards and begged to see the prince. The guards would not wake the prince at such an early hour. At dawn, the brothers turned back into swans and flew away. What else could they do now?

When the chariot came to take Elisia to the prison, she cried, but still she did not utter a word. She climbed into the chariot, still working on the last coat. As the chariot clambered down the street, Elisia saw the 11 swans fly by! They flew up to the chariot and began beating the guards away with their wings. Elisia, now finished with the last coat, threw them upon the swans, and miraculously, they all turned back into men!

The people all thought it was more of her witchcraft, but now, at last, Elisia could speak. She and her brothers told the whole story. At last her brothers were men forever and she was happily married to the wonderful prince. Now she could speak and tell the prince how much she loved him.

The End

THE WOLF AND THE KID, A FABLE (9)

One day a baby goat was eating in a pasture. Some people call a baby goat a kid. Along came a wolf and he pounced upon the baby goat. "You are not long for this world, little kid. You will surely make a nice supper for me!" whooped the wolf.

The kid looked very sad and said to the wolf, "Since I do not have long to live, please at least let my last few moments be merry. Will you sing me a little song and let me dance a few steps?" the little kid begged.

The wolf thought it might be nice to have a little music before his supper and he granted the kid's wish and began to play on his flute. Then he started singing. The kid danced and twirled around making the wolf think he must be very good at singing. The kid continued to dance and clap his hands and the wolf sang louder and louder.

The man who watched the goats soon heard the music making and merriment and ran up and chased the wolf away.

The wolf ran off, very angry at himself. He knew that if he had gone on and been the hungry wolf he was supposed to be instead of trying to be a great singer, he would have had his meal.

The End

Moral: Be yourself, and not something you want others to think you are.

THE WOLF IN SHEEP'S CLOTHING, A FABLE (10)

There once was a wolf who could never get his fill of sheep. The shepherd watched so carefully over his flock of sheep, though, that the wolf could never get near enough to catch a sheep.

One day the wolf found a sheepskin that had been cast aside. Wonderful! He put on the sheepskin and wandered into the flock, unnoticed. He spent the whole day trying to decide which sheep he would carry off for his supper that night.

He was still wandering around among the sheep when suddenly they were all herded into a big corral. "Oh, well. Now I shall be able to eat as many as I like while the shepherd is not watching them," he mumbled to himself.

It just happened that the shepherd had, that very day, decided to have lamb chops for his own supper. That evening he came to the corral to find a sheep and the very first one he happened to grab up was the wolf in the sheep's clothing. Of course, it took only one swish of his knife to kill the old wolf.

That just goes to prove that it is often more dangerous for the one that does the deceiving, than for the one that was meant to be deceived.

The End

Moral: It is best to be yourself.

THE WONDERFUL SHEEP (49)

There was once a king with three daughters but the youngest, Miranda, was his favorite. The king had been away for a long time and on his return his daughters had special dresses made to wear just for him. As they all sat down to dinner he asked each girl why she wore that particular color of dress. The eldest said she wore green to signify his fast return. The second wore blue to show that he was as welcome as the sky. The youngest, Miranda, said she wore white because she looked best in white. The reply from Miranda made the king angry. "What arrogance!" he shouted. "But Father, I only wanted to look my very best for you," answered Miranda, surprised that he had not understood her intentions.

Then he asked each one of them what dreams they had while he was away. The eldest dreamed he brought her a new dress that would please him to look upon her. The second dreamed he brought her a spinning wheel so she might weave him fine shirts. Miranda dreamed that on her second sister's wedding day her father held a bowl filled with water for her to wash her fingers in. The king got angry at this. Again that awful arrogance and pride!

That night the king ordered his guard to take Miranda into the forest and leave her there. That she should think he would hold water bowls for her, like a slave, was just too much to bear. The guard took her into the forest and left her in the forest alone, weeping.

Miranda wandered through the forest and came upon a flock of sheep. One sheep was very large and wore pearls around his feet. He wore flowers and a diamond collar around his neck and had a beautiful crown on his head! "Welcome, Miranda," he said. "Tell me why you are so sad." Miranda was shocked. "How did you know my name?" she asked. "Miranda, I have watched and loved you from afar for a long time. I have watched you and your sisters play. Come now and I'll take you where you can rest," said the Wonderful Sheep.

A great chariot, like an oversized pumpkin, drew up with six goats harnessed to the chariot. Miranda and the Wonderful Sheep stepped in and they were off! Soon they came to a cave and it stopped. Everything was so beautiful! Flowers and fountains were everywhere.

"Please stay with us. I will make you happy," said the Wonderful Sheep. Miranda was too shocked at the moment to decide on any matters but agreed to stay for now anyway. "Please tell me about this strange and beautiful place," she begged. And he began his story.

"I was once a great king. A wicked fairy loved me and wanted to marry me. I detested her because of her wicked ways. Since I would not marry her she changed me into a sheep and this is the way I must remain for eight years. All the sheep you see here were once men that displeased the wicked fairy."

Miranda stayed with the Wonderful Sheep and even came to love him. He was so kind and generous with her. He seemed so human. But one day, news came that Miranda's eldest sister was to be married. Miranda wanted to go so badly that the Wonderful Sheep arranged it. Miranda reached the palace just as the ceremony began. And when the ceremony was over Miranda fled to her chariot and was soon out of sight. Her family hadn't even known she was there.

Months later news came that Miranda's second sister was to be married. Again, Miranda begged to go. "Just please hurry back," begged the Wonderful Sheep. "My life would end without you." Miranda promised to hurry back as soon as the ceremony was ended. She reached the palace just in time for the ceremony. When the ceremony ended she fled for the door but the king had seen her. "Please stay and honor us at the wedding feast," he begged. He snatched up a bowl and held it before her. "Rinse your fingers in this water and we shall go in to the feast!" "Oh, Father, my dream did come true - you have offered me a bowl to wash my fingers in." On hearing this, the king recognized his daughter and embraced her. He had missed her terribly and was happy to see her alive and well.

As the evening slipped on, the Wonderful Sheep began to worry. At last he ran to the palace. He knocked on the palace door, but no one would let him in. They had heard about this Wonderful Sheep, and hoped that Miranda would stay here and not go back to him. He knew they would not let him into her life and since he could not bear life without Miranda, he lay down and died.

The next day as Miranda set out to see all her friends in town she passed through the palace door. There lay the Wonderful Sheep, dead. She threw herself upon him and cried bitterly. She knew that if she had kept her promise and returned right away he would not have died. No one can live happily ever after if they cannot keep their word.

The End

TOADS AND DIAMONDS (67)

There was once a widow with two daughters. The oldest daughter was much like her mother, both in ugliness and bad temperament, but the younger daughter was very pretty and sweet. The mother spoiled the elder daughter since they were so much alike. The younger daughter was made to eat in the kitchen alone and do all the work. Among her daily chores, she had to go to the fountain a mile from home to get fresh water. One day, as she was filling her pitcher, a poor beggar woman appeared and begged for a drink. "Oh, surely, but first I will rinse my pitcher for you," said the pretty girl. She rinsed the pitched and dipped some water from the clearest spot in the fountain. The beggar woman, having refreshed herself, said, "You are such a sweet and mannerly girl that I will give to you a gift which will be most precious. Every time you speak, either a diamond or a flower shall come from your mouth."

After the girl went home, she could not speak without a diamond or a flower coming from her month! The mother was amazed! "Why does this happen?" the mother cried in joy. The young daughter then told her mother what had happened at the well.

Her mother thought this should also happen for her oldest daughter, so she told her to go the fountain and give water to the beggar woman. The elder daughter was mad. She had never had to fetch water before. She muttered and grumbled, but her mother insisted she go. "Just give the beggar woman water and she will make diamonds come from your mouth, too!" the mother pleaded.

So she went, though not without grumbling. She had no sooner arrived at the fountain than a beautiful lady like a princess came up to her. Actually the princess was the same fairy that had appeared to the younger daughter, but she could not always appear the same way or people would soon know her and be on the watch. "May I have a drink?" the princess asked. Thinking the beggar woman might be watching from a distance, the girl decided she should at least appear to be mannerly and give the princess a drink--but she didn't have to be nice about it. No one was around to hear. "If you must drink, do so quickly and be gone. I am not one of your servants."

"My, what bad manners you have," said the princess. "Your manners are so bad that I am going to show all the world what you are really like. Ever after, when you speak, toads will come from your mouth!"

The unmannerly daughter ran home to her mother, crying, but every time she tried to speak, toads came from her mouth. The mother could not stand such things in her house and chased the elder daughter out. She was so mad at the younger daughter for bringing this about, she chased her out of the house, too.

The poor young daughter ran into the woods where a prince found her crying. He asked why she was crying there alone in the woods. "My mother has chased me away," answered the pretty young girl. As she spoke, diamonds and flowers tumbled from her mouth. The prince was astounded! He took her to his father, the king, and told him the story. The king said she could stay with them. It was not long before the girl and the prince fell in love and they were married and lived happily ever after.

The End

TOM THUMB (11)

One night, Merlin, the great magician, stopped at a peasant's house for supper. They treated him kindly and fed him well, but they were such a sad couple. "Why are you so sad?" the Magician asked. "We are a happy couple, even though we are poor, but we want a son so badly. We would be happy even if our son was no bigger than my thumb," said the husband. Well, Merlin was a great magician, so knowing about these things, he promised them they would soon have a son. And he was right! In good time, the couple had a son that really was no bigger than his father's thumb! So, of course, they named him Tom Thumb.

They were so happy with their new son, even if he was tiny. Tom grew up in age, but never in size. He always stayed the size of his father's thumb. His father prided himself in teaching Tom how to get along in the world. Life can be rough for someone so small.

One morning Tom's mother was making a pudding. Tom climbed up on the bowl to watch and slid down into the pudding. His mother didn't see Tom and kept right on stirring. Tom was nearly drowned with all the stirring and jumped up and down, yelling and screaming! His mother thought the pudding was bewitched and threw it out the window. Boy did Tom need a bath!

Another day Tom went with his mother to milk the cow. The cow thought he was a morsel of food, lapped him up into her mouth. Tom yelled and screamed, and the frightened cow, not knowing what sort of wild thing was in her mouth dropped Tom and he scurried away quickly! He was a bit bruised up from that!

One time Tom was out playing. A bird saw the wee boy and picked him up. Tom yelled and kicked and the bird dropped him into a lake below and a fish gobbled him up! One of the king's servants was out fishing and caught the fish that had swallowed Tom. When the cook cut the fish open, out stepped Tom! She was delighted and ran to show him to the king who fell in love with the tiny boy. He gave Tom the run of the castle and told him to take as much money as he could carry home to his poor parents. The king had a new set of clothes made for Tom and gave him a needle to carry as a sword! Tom was really proud of himself when he carried home a huge silver piece to his parents from the king's treasury.

The End

WHY THE SEA IS SALT (23)

Many years ago there lived two brothers, one very rich and one very poor. On Christmas Eve the poor brother went to his rich brother and asked for a bit of food. The rich brother, since it was Christmas Eve, very reluctantly gave him some bacon. On the way home the man came upon a lady who said she was hungry. The man at once gave her part of his bacon with a smile. "Since you are a kind and generous man, I will help you now," said the lady. "Take your bacon to an oak tree three miles from here. You will find many elves. They will try to buy your bacon, for they love bacon and cannot get any from their magic hand mill. Trade the bacon only for their little hand mill. But make sure they explain how you are to use it."

The man did as he was told. The elves clustered around him and all agreed to trade their little hand mill for the bacon. When he learned how to work it, he hurried home to his wife.

"Wife, come see what I have!" he cried. He turned the handle on the little hand mill and told it to lay a grand meal before them. And it did! It ground out hams, cakes, potatoes, breads, cookies and all sorts of good foods! They had more than enough for a fine feast. They hid the little hand mill behind the door.

In a few days they invited the whole town to a party. The rich brother asked his poor brother where he had gotten all the food when only a few days before he had come begging. The poor brother, did not want anyone to know of the little hand mill for fear of it being stolen. He did not say anything until he drank too much Christmas Cheer, and then he told his brother.

The rich brother begged to buy the little hand mill and at last they made a bargain that it would be sold to the rich brother for 300 pounds when harvest time came. So the man and his wife kept the little hand mill busy for the next few months, grinding out enough food and clothing to last them for many years. Finally harvest time came, and when the rich brother handed over the 300 pounds, he was so excited he didn't even wait around long enough to learn how to work it.

The rich brother ran home and sent his servants outside telling them he would make dinner. Then he sat down and turned the handle and said to the little hand mill, "First, let us start the meal with some fish and soup." The little hand mill began at once to grind out the fish and soup. When he thought he had enough he told the little hand mill to stop. But it did not stop! It ground the fish and soup out so fast that it began to splash down over the bowl onto the floor. He pulled and twisted at the little hand mill, but nothing would make it stop! The soup ran from the kitchen into the parlor. Soon the house was filled with soup and the man thought he might drown! He finally opened the doors and let it run into the fields. Then he ran to his brother's house. "Brother, make this little hand mill stop, and I will give it and your money back!" So the poor man swam through the fish and soup back to the little hand mill and he shut it off.

The poor brother then took the little hand mill home with him and put it back behind the door. One day his wife begged for a new house. Now they had the little hand mill, so they may as well look rich as well as eat rich! So they bid it grind out a beautiful home by the sea. The walls on the outside were made of gold and glistened for miles. Men on ships often stopped to admire it.

One day a sea captain, who reaped salt from the sea to sell on the market, heard about this fine house and the little hand mill inside it. He stopped to visit with the owners of the house, but before he left, he stole the little hand mill. Never again would he have to sail the seas to find salt. He took his ship far out to sea and said to the little hand mill, "Grind salt!" and the little hand mill began to grind out salt. It ground out so much salt so fast that the ship began to groan under the weight of the salt and the captain told the little hand mill to stop. But the little hand mill just kept right on grinding out salt! No amount of fumbling with the knobs could make it stop. Finally the ship sank with the captain, the salt, and the little hand mill, and to this day the little hand mill is at the bottom of sea and is still grinding out salt. And THAT is why the sea is salt!

The End

Made in the USA
Middletown, DE
14 July 2023

35105544R00100